THE OASIS WITHIN

Best Wishes!

THE
OASIS
WITHIN

TOM MORRIS

A Journey of Preparation

A Short Companion to the Series
Walid and the Mysteries of Phi

WISDOM WORKS
Published by Wisdom Works
MorrisInstitute.com

Published 2015

ISBN 978-0-692-50047-7

Printed in the United States of America

Set in Adobe Garamond Pro
Designed by Abigail Chiaramonte

To my fellow travelers
in search of wisdom.

CONTENTS

I

THE OASIS WITHIN

EGYPT. MANY YEARS AGO.

It was late in the day, not long beyond the summer solstice of 1934. But out across the endless sand, the date on a calendar was of little relevance. This part of the world had its own rhythms.

The sun had just set. Evening was beginning to cool the desert oasis. A small fire popped and sizzled. The old camel driver leaned back on brightly colored blankets rolled up behind him and stacked against the base of a tree. He took a straw out of his mouth, turned to the boy sitting with him, and said, "My friend, I'm glad you could come along on the caravan this time."

"I am, too." The boy paused for a moment and added, "I'm sure you know this, Uncle, but I've enjoyed everything about the trip so far, even on the hard days."

"Good. That's what I had hoped for you."

"It's all so new to me. And I love this oasis."

The old man smiled. "I do, too. The time we have for rest here will give us more of a chance to talk in depth, the two of us."

"I'm glad."

"There are some things I need to tell you, some ideas I want to share, and make sure you understand."

"Really?"

"Yes. I've been watching you with great pride during these first days of our journey. I'm now confident that you're old enough at this point, and can be given some insights that will be important tools for what lies ahead. I've been waiting to share these thoughts with you." A slight smile crossed his lips. "I believe the time has come for you to learn some new things."

The boy stopped scooping sand in his hands and sat up a bit. "What do you want to tell me? I'm eager to hear it."

"Excellent. We can start with something simple and powerful."

"Ok. Good."

The old man stroked his short beard and collected his thoughts for a moment. "We're indeed on a special journey together right now. And there's a big picture for what we're doing. It's an important truth about how we should live in the world."

He paused for a couple of seconds more, and then said, "Life is supposed to be a series of adventures. Think of this trip itself. On some difficult days, we cross the desert for what seems like forever. Time moves almost reluctantly—slowly, and heavily, as if weighed down by the heat of the sun and mired in the sand. On other days, we may catch a refreshing breeze, and even be at a delightful oasis like this one, with good food and drink, abundant water, and new friends. We tell stories. We sing and dance. We play games. We read. We enjoy ourselves. Time is different. The days here can pass far too quickly. But they prepare us well for the next stretch of travel."

He went on. "You know, I've been on many caravans before, and on days of scorching sun, we wish for shade. Then, when clouds of wind and sand come to block the sun and we can barely see beyond the nose of the camel, we wish for clear skies again. The young men say, 'We can't survive a storm!' But the same ones earlier said, 'We can't endure this sun!' We do endure and survive. And when we arrive at places like this, we rejoice. The difficulty of the travel and its pain vanish like a mirage of water on hot sand. And we're refreshed."

The boy replied, "I know what you're saying. Some of the travel has been harder than I had guessed. Our second day seemed long."

"It did."

"And I had a few tough days back at home, in the village, not long ago when time wanted to crawl along. But it's good to be here now. This oasis is great. It relaxes me, and it gives me a sense of peace."

The old man nodded his agreement. He spoke softly. "The real secret to life is to carry in your heart an oasis every day, a place of rest and refreshment within you. Then, when the sun is intense, or if storms lash out, you can have a measure of what you feel right now, under these stars, surrounded by these swaying palms, eating these figs, and enjoying your cool drink. The oasis within is always yours, if you'll take it with you."

The boy thought for a moment. He looked a bit puzzled and then gazed up at the face of the old man he had long admired, with all its familiar wrinkles, and, knowing well the wisdom that must lie behind these words, he asked, "But, how can I do that? I'm not sure what you mean. How can I take an oasis with me wherever I go?"

"With your thoughts, dear boy. All the power we have starts with our thoughts. Use your thoughts well, and you create within you the most vital thing you'll need for life's journey. Your thoughts can have great power—very great, indeed. Use them well each day and you'll cultivate your own oasis within."

"Can you tell me more about how to do this, about how it works?" The boy sounded eager to learn something new and useful.

"Gladly. Consider the old camel we have with us. In the sun, he's calm. In a storm, he's calm. Here, tonight with us in this new place, he's calm. It's hard to excite or alarm him at all. In his mind, he lives in the moment and carries on, regardless of what he faces."

"But Uncle, maybe he doesn't understand life like we do. We know how things can happen to hurt us, and that's why we're scared, or worried, or sad. He doesn't see things the same way."

The old man smiled. "In a sense, that's exactly my point."

The boy looked slightly perplexed again.

The old man asked him, "Have you ever come across a telescope?"

"Yes, once, in the village, years ago. There was a man, a visitor, with a small telescope that you could hold in your hands, and he let me look through it. Things that were far away suddenly seemed close. It was like magic."

The old man said, "When I was a lot younger than you, a kind neighbor gave me such a telescope as a gift. I imagine it was much like the one you held. I used it to look all around me. I remember I once stood in the middle of the village with it. I could see people in their houses, men at a distance, and animals far down the road. I discovered something important that day."

"What was it?"

"When I peered through the small end like everyone does, it made things look bigger and closer. But then, I turned the telescope around in my hands. I have no idea what made me think to do that. I put it up to my eye again and gazed this time through the big end. I was so amazed! It made everything around me look much smaller and far away. Large men seemed little. Tall trees were shrunken into tiny images of themselves." He smiled at the memory.

The boy said, "I never looked into the big end like that."

"Well, we all have in our minds something like an inner telescope for our thoughts and feelings. When things seem bad, we automatically view them through the small end of our telescope, like most people do, and then those things look much bigger and closer and worse than they really are. That's what makes us frightened or worried. But, just like a real tele-scope, we can turn it around, and look through the other end. That will make our problems appear smaller. It will reduce in our minds and hearts the perceived size of what we face. Then we can feel bigger and more powerful. Often, that's just what we need."

"Wow. That makes sense. It's a new way of thinking."

"Yes it is. So, when you're afraid or worried or sad, think of your inner telescope. Are you looking through the end that almost everyone uses? Are you making things seem bigger and more imposing than they really are? You have the power to turn the telescope around and gaze through the other end. You'll then see the difficulties as smaller, and you'll feel better, and stronger."

The boy was impressed, and pleased. "I like this idea. It's a good image. And really, it's not something I've ever thought about."

The old man smiled again. "Here's the ultimate secret, my boy. Once you've mastered this trick with your mind and understand the power of perspective, once you've grown enough in wisdom and knowledge of the world, you can put your inner telescope down and simply look at things as they are. And you'll know. Most things in reality are no bigger than we can handle. And that's important to remember."

The boy thought for a few seconds. Then he said, "I guess the camel stays calm because he feels big and sees most things as small, or at least, no bigger than he can handle."

"Yes. That's his way. And it's healthy for him to have that perspective. He's a wise creature in this regard. Wisdom in life is almost always about perspective. Choosing the right point of view, and seeing things properly, gives you power, because it brings peace to your heart and calm to your mind. Then you can think clearly and act well, even in challenging times."

The boy had a serious look on his face, one almost of contemplation. "I think I understand what you're saying. I heard a few of the men the other day talking about troubles in the kingdom. I remember that one of them said, 'We live in difficult times.' Another man then responded, 'Yes, but if we take the right perspective, they may be just the times we need.' I didn't really know what he meant, but I thought that this was an interesting thing to say. The first man seemed worried. The second man sounded calm and confident."

"You're right. There's a big difference. It's ultimately our thoughts that make us feel good or bad, worried or confident. Our thoughts can cause us to feel victimized by circumstances, or else prepared for action. And here's the most important thing to remember: We can learn to control our thoughts in this regard, with practice, and effort, until finally it becomes more natural, and almost effortless, like the way we breathe. When we govern our thoughts well, using the power of the mind, we clear the path for our journey in life to be a good one."

"That makes a lot of sense."

"Good. I'm glad. And there's one more thing. Think of the camel again. He lives in the present moment. He doesn't worry about the future or the past—what may come, or what's gone. Most people make a big mistake and do the opposite. They turn their inner telescopes toward times that don't exist. They seek to peer into the future, endlessly guessing what's next and worrying, or hoping; or else they spend too much time trying to relive the past, or dwelling on it in a negative way and regretting it, or feeling anger about it. But when they do this, all they see are things that don't exist now, in this moment. The past is gone and the future has not yet come."

"That's true. But don't we often have to think of other times?"

"Yes. But not obsessively. We should certainly learn from the past, using the knowledge it has brought us, and we need to plan for the future, doing our best to make it good. But consuming yourself with times you don't inhabit, letting your heart rise and fall, overcome with good or bad feelings about what you think you see back in the past or out in the future, that can make problems for how you live right now."

"Then, why do so many people live like this?"

"Memory is powerful. And the imagination is strong. Memory can tie us to the past. Imagination can push us to the future. But without truly living in the present, paying attention to it, and knowing it as it is, we can never properly interpret the past or create the best future."

The old man paused and then suddenly had a big smile on his face. He said, "A person is truly blessed who can live with his heart immersed in the one, rich, deep and wide moment that alone is now real. He gives himself the best chance in this life for happiness and great deeds. That person takes his oasis with him wherever he goes."

The boy picked at the leather of his sandal as he thought about this, and then he summed it all up, to make sure he understood it: "So, then, part of taking my oasis with me through life means living most fully in the present moment, and part of it means choosing a good perspective and not letting any difficulties look bigger, or worse, than they really are."

"Yes. You're getting the idea. We have many ways of taking an oasis within us wherever we go. These are two of the most important."

2

PREPARING FOR THE JOURNEY

THE NEXT DAY.

There was a nice, light breeze stirring the trees of the desert oasis in the early morning sun. The old man was gathering his supplies, packing up food, and storing water in containers they would carry for the days of travel to come. Others nearby were doing the same. The boy walked up to him. "Uncle, are we leaving today?"

"No. Tomorrow, we leave. Today, we prepare."

"But I really like this place! I wish we could stay a lot longer." The boy had a big smile on his face, as if in anticipation of getting his way and changing their schedule.

The old man laughed aloud. "I know that look! Sit for a moment with me." He smiled broadly as well, put down his bags, gestured toward the ground and sat in the sand. As the boy joined him, he said, "Let me ask you something."

The boy replied, "Sure, ask anything. What can I explain for you?"

The old man laughed again. "I do learn a great deal from you, but right now I want you to think together with me about something."

"Ok. What's the topic?"

"This is my question: What do we do here at the oasis?"

"Well, we eat good food, drink tasty juice, and rest, and have fun. You read, and you sit and talk with your friends. I read some too, but most of the time I've been playing ball with the boys from the other caravan that's here. When I feel like it, I even take naps in the shade."

"Yes, indeed. We're both using the oasis well. We rest and refresh ourselves. We enjoy our time, and restore our energy for the next part of the trip."

The boy smiled and said, "I can tell you're going to explain something to me now."

The old man chuckled. "You're right. You know me well. And here it is. The purpose of any oasis is to assist in a journey. Do you see?"

"Yes, I do. I think. But I bet you're going to tell me more about what that means."

"I am, indeed. If the purpose of the oasis is to assist in a journey, by allowing us to rest and refresh ourselves for the next stage of our adventure, that means we can't just stay here at the oasis, as much as we might want to. The remainder of our travel awaits us. The many good things here have helped prepare us for it."

"Still, a little longer here would be nice."

"Yes, a little longer is fine. So, we'll go tomorrow. We can relax and eat the good food here and drink something pleasant for a bit longer, and then we'll get back to work, which at present is our travel."

The boy now had a sly smile on his face and said, "But, Uncle, let me ask you a deeper question."

"Certainly, my boy. What is it?"

"Why do we work so hard and travel under such a deadline? Why can't we just extend our use of the oasis, for its truly intended purpose? Why not rest and enjoy ourselves as long as we'd like? The desert is patient. It will be there for us when we feel like travel. But for now, more fun and food would be good." At this point, the smile had grown into a big grin and he held his arms outstretched in the air.

That brought a merry laugh from the old man. "These are all good things, my boy. But other and greater things await us. The camel we have enjoys his rest here. But he also needs to walk. If he rested all the time, his legs would not work so well. And soon, he would weaken and even die."

"I didn't know that."

"Yes. And we're a little bit like the camel. We need different things. We need to play and to work, to rest and to be active. We need to enjoy and to accomplish. We need a break from work, and then a return to work. When you have the right balance in your life, it's good, and you feel better. Everyone benefits from balance."

The boy said, "Tell me some more about this, about balance. Is it like when I walk along the rocky edge of a wall? Sometimes, it's easy. Other times, it's harder. Now and then, I fall."

"Yes, it's very much like that. But, first of all, I should tell you that there's no such thing in life as perfect balance."

"What do you mean?"

"Let me give you an illustration. When I was young, I once saw a famous tightrope walker at a circus in a large city. Up in the air, he had a rope pulled tightly between two towers."

"Wait. He walked on a rope in the air?"

"Yes. He did. I saw him make his way from one tower to the other, over the stretched out rope, holding on to a long stick across the front of his body to help him balance. He swayed back and forth as he carefully took each step. His hands dipped right, and then left, his feet shook and lurched and then steadied him with constant movement."

"I've never seen anything like that."

"It was fascinating and fun to watch. And I learned something very important about balance that day."

"What was it?"

"Balance is not a steady, static thing. It's dynamic. It's movement. It's ever changing. The essence of it is care and correction, or awareness and adjustment. It's an ongoing dance of change, moving from one thing to another. This is the dance that engages us all. The famous tightrope walker, the man I watched so closely, was almost always a little out of balance, but he sought to correct himself along the way, every moment, off to the left, then off to the right, and back and forth."

"I see. That's pretty interesting."

"Life is like that. We're never in perfect balance. But attaining basic harmony in this world means being in a process of movement and change, balancing and rebalancing the things you do, the actions you focus on, while keeping a firm hold on what you value. Remember the tightrope and you'll be reminded of what balance in life requires."

The boy stood up quickly, bent his left knee, and placed his weight on his other foot, shifting a bit right, then left, and back and forth, shaking and catching himself as he said, "Like when we talk now and play later, or rest now and work later." Then he dropped down to the sand.

The old man laughed. "Yes, indeed. That's quite dramatic. You have the idea. Some people don't understand this at all. When they're working, they wish they were resting, or playing. When they rest or play, they feel guilty and think they should be working. When they're with family, they're missing their friends. When they're with friends, they're missing family. They're never content with where they are."

The boy leaned back and said, "I've known some older people who act that way. They look like they're never really happy with what they're involved in, and always seem to think they should be doing something else. It's almost like they feel guilty about not being able to do everything at the same time."

The old man agreed. "Yes. Exactly. It's sad. People who feel like this just don't understand that we're always a little out of balance, and that such a thing is fine and normal. Real balance simply means changing and redirecting our energy when the time is right, and turning to whatever other good thing we had not just been doing. We change when change is right. But living always with distraction or regret, guilt or frustration, won't help anything. While you're doing something that's worth your time, you should do it with all your heart. Then, when the moment for change comes, you can go do something else, and feel good in perhaps a new way."

The boy looked at the sand around his feet, then turned

back toward the old man. "So, I think this is what you're saying: Sometimes, we're at an oasis like this, and sometimes we're in the desert, on our journey. We change when we need to change. That's our balance."

"You're right. If we lingered here too long, that wouldn't be good balance. If we traveled in the desert every day without rest, that wouldn't be balance, either. We do what we need to do, and, when we can, what we like to do. And we're always open to change."

He paused for a moment and said, "Whatever is not part of the adventure is preparing us for the adventure, and in the end, that's also a part of the adventure, too!"

At this phrasing of the thought, he spontaneously laughed again. And so did the boy, in response to his uncle, whose wisdom came often in serious words, but then, sometimes, with a joke and a laugh.

"But, Uncle, I have one more question, as long as we're talking about this."

"Ask anything."

"Ok, How do we know when it's time for a change? How do we know when we should switch our focus from one thing to another?"

The old man lifted his hands in front of him, palms up, saying, "How does a bird know when to rise up and fly, and when to land on a tree or a house? How does a fish in water know when to change direction and swim away? Sometimes, it's spontaneous. It's creative. It just happens. These creatures, they simply do what they do when they do it. And, of course, for boys like you, throughout your life, up until now, it's often the same. You play, you run, you eat, and then you come and talk to me. How do you decide what to do and when to do it? You most often just do what you do. You're spontaneous— except, of course, when your mother tells you what to do, and then you must obey her ... immediately!"

"Yes, then I have to change what I'm doing, without hesitation!"

"Indeed! But as you grow older, you begin to sense when the time is right to do something, and then when you should stop doing it, when you should act in one way, and then in another. Like the tightrope walker, you can feel when you're getting too far out of balance, and in need of adjustment, and then you change and adapt, or else you fall, which can hurt. Life is about timing, and a sense of what's right. You come to understand when it's the right time for a change, for doing something different. As you grow wise, you develop an intuition for what's appropriate, and the inner grace to change deftly and well.

"As we mature, we begin to get a feel for the proper ebb and flow of life. When the moment is right for a change, it's like a piece of ripe fruit. The experience will be best if taken then. But when we feel we should change what we're doing, and we resist the feeling with no good reason—just out of habit or comfort or groundless fear—we often find that we end up dissatisfied and unhappy. That teaches us to follow our sense of when something new is needed."

"I see."

"And yet, there's one important caution to add."

"What do you mean?"

"We should never allow temporary feelings, however

intense, to push us into big or permanent changes that might not be right for us. When it comes to very important things, only our deepest feelings, our strongest intuitions, linked together with our highest values, can guide us well. Whenever we feel like change, but great things are at stake, we should test our feelings to make sure they reflect the best of who we are. Then we can respond wisely and well."

The boy looked up at the sky, and pondered this for a moment. It was a lot for him to take in. He finally concluded, "So, Uncle, you say we should learn to respond wisely to our feelings. They can't always be trusted, but they can guide us well if they truly reflect who we are?"

The old man nodded. "Yes, my boy. We allow our most appropriate feelings to guide us whenever that's possible. But, there's one more consideration to mention, and it relates to our situation now."

"What's that?"

"Sometimes, we have a schedule we've planned in advance, based on firm commitments and promises we've made, and we should stay true to the plan unless we have a compelling reason to depart from it. That's how it goes for the journey we're on right now. We need to arrive in the city and get our things to market by a certain day. And there are people to see. We've made promises and agreements. When we feel like resting, and rest is possible, then we do so, but only as long as our schedule allows. Then, we go on, as planned."

The boy said, "I understand. But, as long as we're talking like this about things, I have another question, and maybe it's a big one."

"Ok, a big one is fine. I promise to search for a suitably large answer."

The boy flashed a grin and then grew serious again. "Why do we ever make plans at all? This may sound silly, but why not just be spontaneous, like birds and fish, and little kids?"

The old man nodded his head. "You're quite a philosopher."

"Yes, like you."

"It's a very fine thing. And I do have an answer for you. It's good to be spontaneous when we can be. But, plans allow us to make different and worthwhile things happen. They're necessary whenever we're seeking difficult outcomes. They make it possible for us to live and work with other people. When we honor our plans, others know they can count on us. That way, we can work well together and prosper."

"Yes, but how do you make yourself stick to a plan or a schedule when you really don't feel like it? That's sometimes a problem for me. I know you have great self discipline. But, how do you manage it?"

"We all have feelings and desires that come and go. This is why I speak of following our deepest and most proper feelings, not just any emotion or inclination that crosses your heart. Like you, I have a good feeling of enjoyment in this place. I'd love to stay for many more days. But I also have deeper feelings of commitment to our schedule, and to all the people who are depending on us. I know that doing what I've promised represents who I am, and it will make me feel best in the end. I've learned to put aside immediate temptation for the sake of long term good. It's not an easy thing to master, but it's one of life's most important skills. And it brings the deepest satisfaction."

The boy smiled and said, "I remember when you first promised to bring me on this trip. I was looking forward to it for weeks. And then, when the day came that you told me to pack my bags and get ready, I was really excited, and glad."

The old man said, "It was important to you that I keep my promise and stay true to the plan we had made."

"Yes, it was." He looked thoughtful for a few seconds, and confided, "It's not always easy being an only child, you know, without any brothers or sisters around. And, mom and dad have both been extra busy this year. You've also gone on lots of trips, and that's been hard for me, too. I haven't even seen my friends who live nearby as much as I normally do. It's been a bit of a lonely time."

The old man said, "Yes, we've had a difficult year in many ways."

"So, every time you've come back from one of these trips and I've heard all the stories you tell, I've imagined these caravans being full of great friendship and good talk for all the men traveling together. It's something I've really wanted to experience. Having a chance to be part of this trip, knowing I was going to come along, and making all the plans for it that were necessary, has kept me going recently, through some of the harder days."

The old man replied, "I'm glad. All the men enjoy your company. I know it's been tough for you recently. So many of us have stayed busy, and we have indeed been away far more than usual. This trip is a chance for us to be together while I still get vital work done, a time that both of us have needed. We travel with many purposes. Promises have been made, and they also must be kept."

"I understand."

"There will be some busy days in the capital city and we may not have as much time together then as we do now, at least, at first. But you'll find many things to enjoy there while I work."

He stroked his beard twice, thought for a moment and said, "Now, let me get back to your original question about why we make plans. Some journeys in life are spontaneous. Others are laid out in advance. But even well planned endeavors can often have a good measure of spontaneity woven through them. Some adventures have one purpose. Others have many. But whatever good purposes we have should all be respected. Would you agree?"

"Spontaneously!" the boy said, and made his uncle laugh.

"Good! And you know, most often, the self discipline of sticking to what we've freely agreed to do is not such a hard thing, as long as we remember that it will likely satisfy us the most in the end. And so, we need to have the inner strength to end our visit and leave this oasis tomorrow, however much we'd like to stay. We can't linger too long at this pleasant place, because if we did, we'd break our promises to others, and end up out of balance, as well."

The old man stood up, and so did the boy, who said, "I agree. Balance is a good thing. And doing what we promise is important."

"Yes, both these things are crucial. So, enjoy this day here to the fullest. Make the time count. Tomorrow we'll leave, at least for now. But we may visit here again." He smiled and said, "And, remember, we can always take an oasis with us wherever we go, in our hearts and our minds."

The boy also smiled. "Yes, Uncle, I remember. I'll also begin to make my own preparations today for the trip tomorrow. For the moment, though, if you would, please excuse me. I've truly enjoyed our talk, but my deepest feelings are telling me that it's time for one of those changes you described. I need to go now and kick a ball with my new friends. Otherwise, I could lose my overall balance and fall off the tightrope."

The old man was impressed with his student and smiled once more at his cleverness. "Yes, I agree that it's important for you to resume your play now. You may go—and, of course, for the sake of good balance."

They both grinned and, with his uncle's blessing, the boy jogged back across the sand toward distant sounds of merriment. It was a good time for some final enjoyment. The course of their upcoming travel would soon enough bring with it a demanding situation that would involve both a dangerous turn of events and a frightening challenge.

3

A BEAUTIFUL MORNING

IT WAS A GREAT MORNING.

The air was thoroughly pleasant for the men and animals. A light breeze kept everyone feeling refreshed.

The day had come for the old man and the boy, along with their caravan, to leave the oasis, where the two of them had begun to talk of important things, and return to their travel across the desert. The next day had then come and gone as well. And now, the morning of a third day was dawning, as the line of camels and men walked on.

When the sun rose higher into the sky, the sand began to glow around them in all directions. They would soon have to stop, as they did each day, pitching simple tents for shelter against the more intense heat that would rule the next few hours.

The first day out of the oasis had been uneventful. The boy mostly rode. His uncle rode some, but walked more. The second day had been hotter and harder. But the start of this third day came with a measure of coolness they hadn't felt since the shade of the oasis.

They were on two camels this morning, riding side-by-side. The boy looked over at his companion and said, "Uncle, it feels like this will be a good day for us. It's so pleasant. The travel is easier already. I think everything will go smoothly for us."

"Perhaps, my boy. We'll see. Things are not guaranteed to be as they at first seem. But that's fine. We'll always make the best of whatever comes our way."

"Yes. That's something you've been teaching me. I have to remember that things often look different from what they really are."

The old man replied, "We learn to question appearances. And sometimes they give us their secrets." Then he put his finger to his lips as if guarding his own secret, and smiled.

The boy smiled back. "I like what you say. We'll always make the best of whatever comes our way."

"Yes. Remember this: We can't control the day, but only what we make of the day."

The boy nodded. He recalled one of the main ideas in their previous talks, and raising a finger into the air, he said, "Our power is in our thoughts!" He spoke more loudly now over a slightly stronger wind that was beginning to come across the sand.

His proud teacher replied, "With our minds, we determine much of our experience. And we can learn from anything the world gives us."

They rode on for nearly an hour more, and continued to talk, now and then, speaking of whatever came to them. Then, in the midst of a sentence, the old man turned his head and paused as he heard the call to rest conveyed by the camel drivers up ahead. "It's time for us to stop and pitch our tents. Let's hop down and make preparations."

He brought his camel to a halt and, even as the animal was kneeling, dismounted with one fluid movement. He then reached up to his nephew, who slid down smoothly with just a little support. Loud words and a bustle of activity ran up and down the camel train as the men began to ready things for their mid-day rest.

But, at the very next moment, there was a sudden mighty booming howl of wind and a blast of sand that lashed them all. The boy tasted a mouthful of grit and felt a sharp sting on his skin that unleashed a twinge of primal fear inside him. Men shouted more and pointed to the distance, behind them, where an ominous and fast moving darkness was now to be seen, coming in their direction.

At once, all the animals began to lie down where they were, in positions of instinctive protection. "Quickly!" the old man called out above the noise. "Get next to your camel, on this side, opposite the approaching darkness!"

"Uncle Ali! What is it? What's happening?" The boy showed an emotion of alarm across his face.

"A storm. A windstorm is moving in." The old man reached to take the boy's arm.

"What can we do?"

"We use what we have. We stay calm. And we move quickly."

He guided the boy to crouch down on his hands and knees, and then lean forward, tightly positioned up against the side of the camel. "Cover your face. Protect your head. Look away from the wind. Close your eyes. Breathe only through your scarf." His words were calm but firm.

"This is scary!" The boy's muffled voice could barely be heard.

"It's good to feel fear, if it helps us act quickly and well. Now, it's our job to be strong, to be at peace, and wait."

The noise was so loud, and the pain of the sand so striking that the whole of nature seemed to be coming down on them in a smothering attack. Seconds felt like minutes, and minutes were magnified beyond all measure. The old man held the body of the boy tightly.

When the great wind subsided, every camel was at least partly buried in sand. But none was lost. As the men began getting out of their protective positions and standing up, shaking the sand from their robes and other items of clothing, it became clear that all of them had survived the onslaught as well. One driver, a strong looking friend of the old man, came over to check on him and the boy.

"Ali! Are you and Walid all right?" The robust younger man helped dislodge them from the weight of the sand now almost packed around them.

"Yes, Hakeem, my friend. It seems we're both blessed to be fine." Ali helped the boy to his feet, and began to brush the sand off his robe. "This young man just experienced his first major storm in the desert. And, with quick action, using what we had, we both survived it quite well."

The boy coughed and had to spit some sand out of his mouth. The old man handed him a small canteen of water and said, "Rinse and spit again. Don't swallow." Walid swished the water around in his mouth and expelled the small hard particles of grit. Ali then put a hand on one of his shoulders and said, "You were brave, my boy. You acted well, and you're now safe."

"I didn't feel brave," he said with a sense of shame. "I was scared."

Hakeem spoke up and replied, "You don't have to feel brave to be brave. It's about how you act, and what you do. Your uncle's right. You were brave. It's natural to feel scared in the face of danger. A coward is frozen in fear or tries to run away. You did what needed to be done. And I'm glad to see that you're both fine, as a result. Now, I should go clean the sand off my own camel." He smiled and nodded.

Ali smiled as well and said, "Thanks for your concern, my friend."

Walid said, "Yeah, thanks!" Then he turned to the old man.

"I have to admit, I'm so embarrassed that I thought this would be a good day! I had no idea that such a storm would come along, and so soon after my positive words!"

"No worries, my boy. There's no need to feel bad. It's indeed a very good day ... to be alive and once again breathing clean air—or, at least, so it seems to me!" The old man smiled.

The boy looked surprised and laughed. "Yes! It's a very good day, to still be alive and once more breathing clean air!"

As they began to tend to their camels, Ali said, "We can't always know when storms will come, but using what we have, acting quickly, and keeping peace in our hearts, we can endure them. And then, when the storm passes, it can still be a good day."

The boy nodded and said, "Thanks, Uncle, for what you did to help me through the danger, and, because of your words, learn even more about life. You always teach me something useful."

The old man smiled and now began brushing himself off. He looked at the boy and said, "The world teaches me something every day. When you pay attention to life, truly pay attention, many good lessons come your way. Some arise out of darkness and wind. A mighty tempest can teach us in unforgettable ways. I wager that you'll never forget this brief and violent storm today, and what you learned about how to act quickly, to protect yourself, to stay calm, and endure."

"That's for sure!"

"The most tempestuous things in life often carry with them the deepest and most useful lessons about our actions, and our abilities. If we use our minds well, we can learn from even the most fearful and difficult events. Often, we gain our best insights from precisely those things. And experiencing them can make us stronger."

Walid bent down to scoop sand from his camel, following the lead of his uncle, and he replied, "I'm learning a lot, for sure. And I like the lessons, even when they come from something difficult. In fact, what you've told me just now has already changed my view on the storm."

"Good. We properly seek to avoid storms when it's possible. But if one comes upon us suddenly, like this one did, we deal with it the best we can. And as a result, we grow. Any tempest of life can bring growth, when we react properly."

"What do you mean?"

"Consider the trees of the oasis we just enjoyed, and of our village back home. The ones that have lived through storms are forced to send their roots deeper, for support. They become stronger, as a consequence of what they've endured. They grow sturdy. Other plants that have never been exposed to storms can have shallow roots, and they seem also fine. But if a storm does come along, it's only the trees and plants with deep and extensive roots that will fare well. Those that survive the storm are often made stronger as a result. The same is true of us."

"I see. That makes sense. But surely storms weaken and destroy some plants and trees."

"They do. The result will depend on the strength of the storm, and on how the plant responds. There are indeed some tempestuous events in life that are too overwhelming to survive, in this world. Such things happen. But there are many more whose aftermath depends entirely on how we respond. Do we go deep? Are we resilient? Can we keep hope alive? Do we take proper action? Can we help each other? All these things matter."

Walid paused and said, "That seems right."

The old man displayed surprising speed and strength as he scraped more sand away from the boy's camel, and then his own. When they both stood back up, Ali patted the beast to signal that he should stay in place for the time of rest. He then took a moment to look around at all the other men with their animals, and returned his kind gaze to the boy. He said, "Keep this main lesson well in your mind: We can't control the day, but only what we make of the day. And we'll always make the best of whatever comes our way—even if it's a quite tempestuous turn of events."

The boy said, "Even if it's stinging sand that comes our way and inserts itself into almost every part of our bodies!" And he bent over and vigorously shook his hands through his hair, creating his own miniature sand storm.

The old man then also had to spit out some grit and said, "Even the sand! And, you know, I do believe our skin has been sandblasted cleaner and smoother than it's been for a while. I may even have lost a few of my wrinkles in the storm. I bet I look younger, as a result."

Walid laughed. And they both smiled.

4

DANGER IN THE SAND

AFTERNOONS CAN BE EVENTFUL TIMES.

"Uncle! Uncle Ali!" The boy ran up from a noisy group of several men gathered around something in the sand that was up ahead by about the distance of nine or ten resting camels.

"What is it, my boy?" The old man rolled over from his light nap in the tent and gestured for his nephew to come in.

"A snake! A viper! The others have found it and killed it!" The boy crouched and entered as he spoke, and went down on his knees in the sand. It was late afternoon, and they would set out shortly for a few more hours of trekking toward their destination.

The old man sat up and yawned and wiped his eyes. He commented, "The viper is dangerous. There are not many around here. In this area, there are mostly harmless snakes that eat rats, and keep them from getting into our food when we stop."

Walid replied, "I heard one of the men say that the viper is very deadly. I've seen some of the harmless snakes before. This one looked different." The boy's words tumbled out. He then lingered for a moment in thought, and said, "But here's a question I've never heard anyone ask or answer: Why are there snakes that hurt and snakes that help? That just seems odd." He then sat down more comfortably inside the small tent, with an expectant look on his face.

"Ah. We must do some philosophy. You ask good questions."

"Thanks. I'm always curious about things."

"That's an important quality to have. Now, on your question: Many things can be helpful to us or harmful. Consider the sun. Without it, there could be no life. But it also can kill. Water will nourish you or drown you. Fire can cook your food or burn you to death. A sharp knife might save you or cut you. And so it goes."

Walid made a face and said, "That's very strange, when you really think about it."

The old man smiled. "You're right, but such is our world, my boy. Many things that have power for good have corresponding power for ill. It's often up to us whether we're helped or harmed by these things with two powers. Do you have a moment for a story?"

"Sure, Uncle. I love your stories."

"Good. Let me then tell you about a man who sought treasure his whole life—gold, silver, other precious metals, and jewels, as well as swords made by master craftsmen, ornate knives, and delicate, expensive artifacts like vases and beautiful small statues. He would go out in the world and do whatever it took to acquire such things, then bring them home and store them in an attic room over where he slept, to keep it all safe, and so he could be near his treasure. As he brought additional valuables home and put them in the attic, the floorboards would creak and groan loudly with the weight. But he continued to want more, and still more, and he worked hard to get it."

Walid said, "I'm not surprised. Gold and silver are rare, and good to have. So is all the other stuff." He was listening intently.

"You're right. They can be very good. But this man never used any of his treasure to do productive things in the world. It wasn't even readily available for daily viewing and enjoyment. He just accumulated more, and stashed it in the attic. One night while he was asleep, the total weight of it all made the floor above him collapse, and he was crushed to death by the precious items he had amassed."

"What a terrible thing!"

"Yes. It was sad. The treasure that could have done great good in the right hands, instead did him grievous harm. If he had used it well, and not just piled it up, if he had acted differently, then the outcome would have been quite different. Again, this is a tale of the two powers. What had great power for good also had great power for harm. It can often be up to us whether things help us or hurt us. We must use the resources of this world, including our own talents and time, wisely and well. We should seek the good and take care to avoid the bad."

The boy thought for a few seconds. "How do you know when something will help and when it will harm?"

"We can't always know. But we often do, from experience —our own, and that of others. We pay attention. We listen. We learn, and we can then be wise in what we do, and properly cautious in the world." The old man sat up and began to put on his sandals. He paused for a moment and then continued.

"Consider the viper out there in the sand. You saw him up close, my boy?"

"Yes, sir, I did."

"He has certain markings that are distinctive. If you think you might forget them, you should go back and look again."

"No, I'll remember. I don't have to go back. It was a little creepy."

"Good. Emotion helps us to remember. So, you'll know how to recognize him now. That will make it possible for you to avoid others like him in the future. But I should also tell you that when he's coming your way in the sand, he's a noisy creature. You can hear the roughness of his skin scraping along as he moves, not quite like any other snake. When you hear that noise, beware, and be safe."

"Is he warning us?"

"In a way, he is. If you pay attention in life, you can often sense harm approaching. Very few dangers appear in the world with no warning at all, even if the warning is slight and gives us just moments in which to act. The man with the great treasure heard the attic floor creaking and groaning under all the weight long before it fell. There are signs. There are indications. Recall the storm we just experienced."

"Yes, we felt the wind rise and saw the darkness approach from a great distance."

"That gave us time to act and protect ourselves. Danger in the world is most often like that. If we're paying attention as we walk through life, we can typically see, or hear, or feel signs when something is not right, and possible harm is near. Then we can act to avoid it. But only if we're using our minds well."

"How can I make sure that I use my mind well in this way?"

"Discipline your thoughts and feelings, my boy. Pay attention. Be alert to your surroundings and mindful of your emotions. Cultivate a keen sensitivity to what's real. Don't allow illusions about things outside you, and false feelings inside you, to blind you to the truth. Make sure you value the right things. Be aware of both what you know, and how much you don't know."

The old man used his finger to trace the shape of a snake in the sand beside his blanket. And then he looked up again at his nephew. He said, "Some men fear nothing, not knowing where true danger may be. Others fear too much, imagining danger when none is at hand. Wisdom finds the right balance of boldness and caution."

He tapped his chest and went on. "Emotions like fear are meant to protect us, but, in a strange way, they can also harm us. Again, that shows the two powers. Our emotions are useful only if we listen as we should, overrule them when needed, and always govern them well. They exist to serve us, but will do so properly only if we train them in the art of good service."

"We can train our emotions?"

"Yes, and we need to, in order for emotion to play a positive role in our lives."

"I thought they just happened to us on their own, and we can't really control how or when they rise up in us. Fear comes, or sadness, or excitement, and it's all just natural."

"Our emotions do happen naturally, but over time we can mold them like a potter molds clay. We can create new habits of feeling, and change old ones. We can learn to govern the occurrence, intensity, duration, and appropriateness of the emotions that arise within us."

"We can do that?"

"Yes. It can take time, but it results in something of great value. We use our minds to teach our feelings how to help and not harm us."

The boy picked at the strap of his sandal. He took all this in and then remembered from the storm the rush of emotions he felt, the almost paralyzing fear, and the importance of taking quick action when dealing with clear danger. That brought to mind a concern and he had to ask about it. "What if there is a true danger, like with a viper, and we see it coming, but we don't act quickly enough?"

"Then, we most often suffer the consequences. If a viper ever bites you, either of two things happens. You suffer greatly and yet live, or you go through terrible pain and then die. In either case, you'll never react slowly to such a danger again. If you ever even see someone bitten by that creature and witness the consequences, I promise, you'll remember it for the rest of your life, and you'll take wing and fly like a startled bird if you have to, in order to avoid a bite yourself."

That got a slight smile from the boy.

The old man sat cross-legged and paused for a moment to think. He said, "Those who look and listen carefully, those who truly pay attention to things in the world, and to the feelings that arise within them, those who live with their minds alert and disciplined, and who remember what they learn, and then take the action that's needed, those are precisely the people who are best positioned to live long and well. Remember that, my boy."

"I should always look and listen carefully, pay attention, be alert and disciplined, and take whatever action is needed."

"Yes, that's correct. And what else have you learned?"

"When I see marks in the sand, or hear the scraping of the viper, or even catch sight of anything that looks like what I saw this afternoon, I'll remember and act fast, and maybe the camel and I will both fly away into the sky!"

At this, he fluttered both his hands into the air, and made himself laugh, as the old man chuckled along with him.

5

A QUESTION ABOUT LIFE

THE EARLY DARKNESS OF A NEW DAY BRINGS UNKNOWN POSSIBILITIES.

A cool morning freshness had quietly crept into the tent to touch their bodies and even their minds long before they had opened their eyes or experienced the consciousness of a new awakening. The old man was first teased from sleep, and took a long, deep breath almost silently under his blanket. Then, not much later, the boy opened his eyes. He heard his uncle move and scratch his arm.

He whispered, "Uncle, are you awake?"

A whisper returned. "Well, let me see. Either I am, or I'm having the most interesting dream, in which you're whispering to me, and I'm responding with surprising intelligence for an unconscious man."

There was a faint laugh, and then words whispered once again. "You can be funny even when you're asleep."

"Actually, I'm quite hilarious in my dreams. It's in waking life that I need some loosening up. And, by the way, it's amusing to me that you're continuing to speak in this way to a possibly sleeping man."

"Well, if you wouldn't mind waking yourself up, I've got something serious I'd like to ask you."

Ali then spoke in a low, normal voice. "Ok, then, no more sleep humor. I'm now officially and fully alert. You may ask anything."

The boy also spoke at this point in more ordinary but hushed tones. "It's just that I've been really wondering about something."

"What is it, my friend?"

"I think about this often, recently, but I've never mentioned it to you before. In the past couple of days, it's been on my mind a lot."

"You know you can always share your thoughts or concerns with me."

"Ok. So, here's the question. For most of history, as I understand it, boys my age have normally followed their fathers' occupations. If your father was a sandal maker, you became a sandal maker. If he was a farmer, you worked with him on the land. But now we, in our time, have much more freedom to choose what work to do. And that brings a problem. How will I know what I'm supposed to do when I get older? And … when will I know it?"

The old man smiled in the darkness and it could be heard in his voice. He said, "Oh, you'll know—I'm sure of that; and when you'll know will be … exactly when the time is right."

"But, how? That's my real question. How will I know?"

Ali rolled over to face the boy and propped himself up on one elbow, as he replied. "I'm happy to tell you that there's a reliable answer to your question. And it starts with a philosophy of life."

"Good. I need to know this philosophy."

"It's simple and it's powerful. I believe that we're all here for a reason. We each have a mission in this world. At some point, your personal mission will present itself to you. You'll still retain the freedom to accept or reject it. It will never force itself on you. But it will come to you as an invitation, and with at least some small inkling, sparked by your talents, that you should embrace the opportunity it offers."

"But what if I don't recognize it for what it is? Or, what if I feel the invitation, as you call it, but out of fear, or maybe uncertainty, I hesitate, and pass it up, and then it's gone forever?"

"People pass up opportunities all the time. But there are two kinds of opportunities. This is important to realize. There are opportunities for particular actions, and opportunities for directions of growth. An opportunity for a particular, very specific action, if not taken, may indeed never come back again. The door, open for just a moment in time, will close. And that's that. If you hesitate too long, you may later come to regret not launching out in action while that particular possibility was available, and when it could potentially bear fruit."

"That's what I'm afraid of."

"But there's more to be said. And this is the most relevant to your concern for identifying your future work. There is a second kind of opportunity. Opportunities for growth and development and service come to us many times. If you miss one, another will find you. Miss that one as well, and there will be a third—and, so on. Opportunities for the direction of your best personal growth will materialize again and again throughout your life. If you reject or miss too many of these, for too many years, you will eventually come to a point when you no longer have the chance to become fully what you could have been. But missing one such opportunity, declining or postponing one invitation alone, or even a couple of them, and perhaps several, will not likely block your way forward to your mission, to the difference that you're here to make in the world. If you're eager to find your path, and truly open to whatever it might be, then I sincerely believe you'll find it. Or it will find you."

Walid said, "I like that way of thinking. It's reassuring, and even comforting to a person my age. Too many people seem worried that they're going to miss their one chance in life—like it's all or nothing."

"Yes. Many people deep in their hearts think of the world as a harsh, unforgiving place, a realm of pervasive punishment: They assume that if you turn down a good opportunity, the world will punish you for your carelessness, or your anxiety, or your hesitation, by denying you a second chance. But that thinking is flawed and based in fear. The world doesn't seek to punish or abandon us when we make a mistake—it's a place, instead, of learning and correction and nearly endless possibilities for growth. Mistakes are a part of the process."

The old man paused and then continued. "If you do

something you should not have done, or if you miss doing something that you should have attempted, things will happen to help you realize that fact, and bring you around and correct you along the way. Circumstances will then lead you to another juncture in the road where you can choose again, but this time with more information and understanding. For most of our mistakes, and especially the ones that we make in charting the direction of our personal lives and work, the world is most often a generous and forgiving place. As long as you're paying attention, and trying your best, and seeking the wise advice of others you trust, you'll be fine."

"But, when my proper future presents itself to me, how will I recognize it as being the right direction for me to take?"

"You'll feel it in your heart. It's that simple. Everything in you, and in your journey on this earth up until then, will have prepared you for meeting whatever is to be your future, or at least the next stage of your future. When it greets you, you'll recognize it as a good friend already. You'll never meet the next step along the way to your best path without sufficient preparation, whether it initially seems to you that you've been prepared enough or not. In fact, you'll often feel in some way unready for precisely the journey that you're to take. The purpose of that feeling is to make you reach deep within and draw on a faith that dares to venture beyond the comfort of what you already know. This helps you to grow in a very important way."

As Walid was listening to his uncle's words, he suddenly came to realize that the first light of day had touched the space in their tent, and that he could now see, however slightly. He smiled within to think that talking with this wise and good man always brought light.

Ali continued, saying, "There's a spirit of things in the world. When you're open in your heart and mind, as you are, my boy, you'll partner up with that spirit and move in your best direction, the direction where you'll feel most fulfilled, most fully you, and where you'll make your most positive impact on the world.

"People sometimes resist their own best future because of, primarily, some form of fear—fear of the unknown, fear of the new, fear of failure, fear of what others will think, or say, and even, strangely, the fear of a success that they're not sure they can handle. Some fear losing the regard of certain people, or losing a place to which they're attached, or even the ownership of, or access to, certain things, or physical objects, that unfortunately have come to define them."

"People let things define them?"

"Yes, they often do. That's a sad fact in our world. We can think we own our possessions, when it's they that have come to own us. A concern about keeping up a certain form of living, or style of life, can prevent a man from following his heart, even when leaving behind those things that constrain him would be not a loss, but a liberation. And, in such a case, holding back from his proper path through a fear of loss will create within him a form of dissatisfaction that nothing can heal until he conquers his fear and takes the risk, or the first real step of faith, in the direction he deeply knows is right for him. When a man does that, he helps to create the best destiny he can have. The same is true, of course, for a woman."

"Do we really have many chances to create our best destiny?"

"Yes. And here's a good illustration. I'm sure you remember your father bringing back that silver kaleidoscope from his trip to Paris."

"I do. It was like a small telescope, but you look into it, rather than through it, and you can see amazing patterns of color and light."

"Indeed. When you first turned this tube of changing patterns, which was, as you say, shaped much like a small, fat telescope, the pieces of colored glass within it configured and then reconfigured into many complex and beautiful shapes."

"They did. I couldn't believe how many different patterns I saw in just a couple of minutes, looking into it and twisting it, as outside light illuminated the show."

Ali nodded and continued his thought. "The world itself is like that."

"What do you mean?"

"This world is like a huge kaleidoscope of ever-shifting possibilities, opportunities, hurdles, challenges, and delights. Time and change turn the tube. There are always new paths forward being revealed, chances for growth, and avenues of action with destinations we can hardly imagine. The patterns are indeed continually altering, and options to advance properly present themselves again and again in different places. So you should never despair of finding your way. Even the worst seeming circumstances can, at times, eventually lead to wonderful opportunities. Trust the process of living and learning. Keep your eyes open. And be sensitive to the tug of your heart

when a path that's right for you may appear. The cosmic kaleidoscope, the tube of changing patterns, will continue to turn."

Walid sat quietly for a few moments and said, "I was just
thinking about that boy who was a few years older than me,
and who visited the house for a time about three months ago."

"I remember him well. He was helping your father with a
job."

"That's right. While he was with us, I heard him tell my
parents that he doesn't know what he's going to do for the rest
of his life. His father works with leather, but he said he doesn't
like it the way his father does. His uncle is in the army, but
he feels no attraction to that. His grandfather tends camels.
He said he's occasionally helped with the animals, but doesn't
really enjoy that, either. He said that people in his family have
been insisting he needs to get serious and figure out what he
wants to do for the rest of his life. Dad told him not to worry,
but to keep experimenting, trying, and learning about new
things."

"That was good advice."

"But, Uncle, the problem seemed to really bother him.
And after I heard him talk about his life in this way, it began
to bother me, too. That's when I really started wondering
what I'm going to do for the rest of my life."

"Many people ask themselves that exact question. And
they don't often deal with it well. Properly understood, there's
only one kind of answer to the question of 'What will I do for
the rest of my life?' And it has almost no connection with a
specific choice of vocation, or any particular way of making a
living."

"Really? What do you mean?"

"I mean this. In its only proper form, the question of what will I do for the rest of my life has simply this answer: I'll live with as much excellence as I'm able. I'll act with kindness, compassion, and love. I'll seek wisdom in all things. I'll be open and understanding. I'll honor what's in my heart. And I'll try always to respect the best in others."

"I like what you're saying. But it's all so broad, so general."

"Yes. And for a reason. Everything else can change. The wisest people realize something important that I've mentioned before. Life is supposed to be a series of adventures. The one we're on at any given time is preparing us for the next one, and often in ways we may not even be able to imagine. We walk the part of the path that we can see. And we do it the best we can. We leave to the future those twists and turns we can't now know or even glimpse. The future has its secrets. It will have its challenges, and its wonders. But they are for their proper time. We're responsible in this moment only for what we know, right here, and right now."

The old man smiled and continued, "When you think about the issue of work, and what's yet to come, you never need to ask yourself what you'll do for the rest of your life. You only need to consider what you'll do next. What's the next stage of your current adventure? Or, what's the next new adventure? All else will be taken care of along the way. There's no need to worry about a thing as big as your entire life. Just take care of your life as well as you can in the moment you're living it, and the rest of your life will take care of itself."

"That makes a lot of sense," Walid responded.

"Good. And when you do find yourself in a serious occupation, the best advice I've ever heard is to keep at the job as long as you love what you're doing and you think you have something distinctive to contribute. If either of those things changes, you should make a change, whether internal or external. That's the way to live your working life well. And, guided by this spirit, you'll never have to suffer with ongoing regrets and unhappiness in what you do. Much of life is flow and change. Happiness embraces the adventure as it happens."

They both sat in silence for a few moments, and then the boy spoke. "These ideas you're sharing with me seem very powerful. Now that I've heard them, I can't imagine going through life without them."

"This is another part of what it means to have an oasis within you. If you have perspectives like these, you will have a place of peace and reassurance deep within yourself, a calm spot, a protection against the worry and stress that plague too many people and wear them down. The right understanding helps to create an oasis within. And we always have the opportunity to cultivate this inner place of power."

"Well, there's one other important opportunity that I think will quickly become available to us this morning, as the kaleidoscope of the world begins to turn with this new day."

"What is it that you have in mind, my friend?"

"The opportunity for breakfast."

"Yes, and it's not one to be missed. Let's get up and go eat!"

6

THE KEYS TO THE KINGDOM

IT WAS NOW LATE EVENING. ANOTHER STRETCH OF TRAVEL
WAS BEHIND THEM.

All the lanterns and fires were out. The many activities of the
day had long ended. A great hush enveloped the tent. Complete
darkness settled gently around the old man and the boy.

Walid was lying on top of his blankets with his eyes still
open. He suddenly spoke in a soft and wistful tone.

"I should have been born a prince." The words hung for a
moment in the air.

"But you were, dear boy—or, should I say, Your Highness?" The answer came quickly.

"I'm serious, Uncle. I would make a great king."

"And you will."

"Quit teasing me." The boy rolled over in the direction of
his friend, feeling both surprised and amused by his unexpected response.

The old man's voice was low and calm. "I'm as serious as you are, young Prince."

"Ha! Is there something my parents have forgotten to tell me all these years, dear Uncle?"

"There are things yet to be revealed."

The boy leaned up on one elbow. He felt like his uncle's words were just too silly, and yet he couldn't help but play along. "Well then, where's my palace, and my kingdom?" He'd get the best of this little exchange. But again, his uncle had a quick answer.

"Your palace tonight appears to be this humble tent. And, if you indeed wonder about your kingdom, you should just look outside the tent. It's plain to see."

The boy got up in mock curiosity and stepped a bit beyond the flap of their simple temporary abode.

"Do you see?" The old man's voice betrayed his smile.

"I see the night sky."

"Describe it to me, Your Highness. Is it just a dark, empty blackness, devoid of all things?"

"No. There are giant balls of fire far away, bright blazes of light scattered all across the darkness, like huge distant campfires that go on forever." The boy's voice was a bit more animated and even tinged with a touch of pretend drama, which strangely began, in a single breath, to shade into a feeling of real drama.

A reply came from inside the tent. "Those are the many villages in your vast kingdom, Sire."

"They're stars, Uncle, and planets." The boy almost laughed again at the old man's inventiveness.

"Yes, yes, indeed, and there's nowhere on earth they flame forth as brilliantly as here in the evening cool of the desert. But you need to know that they represent kingdoms within kingdoms throughout the endless expanse of your royal domain. Oh, and I should point out that the smaller sources of light sparkling overhead are the jewels to be used for your magnificent crown. See how they shine and glitter with a splendor beyond description! We should gather them for you soon. It won't be long before the coronation."

Those words were just too funny. The boy fully took up the spirit of the exchange. "If all this is my kingdom, dear Uncle and High Counselor, then where are my loyal subjects?"

"I'm one, my boy, in this very moment. And there will be many others like me, as numerous as the grains of sand inside this tent, starting right under our blankets and going down to where the desert begins, very deep and far beneath our feet."

"That's a lot."

"Yes. It's a lot."

"Well, then, where are my royal robes, and my scepter, the symbol of my rule? Where are my books of laws and decrees? And how about my armies?"

"There's a simple answer to your questions. And it's true. All of these wonderful things are within the powerful, creative inner sanctum and throne room of your mind, my young Prince."

"You're joking well with me, Uncle."

"No, again, I'm completely serious. You were born to be, and will grow to become, the rightful sovereign of your thoughts, and whatever those thoughts can produce. There's no external limit imposed on the domain over which you can rule on this earth—if you begin properly within your mind, and then continue on as a good man. You were created to reign, and if you rule your own mind and heart with both nobility and humility, you're then ready to take charge of the potentially vast kingdom outside yourself, as well, a realm that eagerly awaits your ascension to the throne."

"What are these qualities, nobility and humility, of which you speak?" Walid asked this question in what he considered to be a theatrical, royal tone. The words were familiar to him, but he wasn't completely sure of their full meaning. And his High Counselor quickly explained.

"Nobility is a sense of your own greatness, and the true greatness of what you rightly value, along with the importance of what you're doing in this world. Nobility comes from inside you. It arises in your soul. It's an attitude and a sensibility that you bring to everything you do, every action, by caring about little things, knowing they're actually big, and attempting big things, knowing that they're never bigger than your calling, your quest, and the adventure for which you're here."

"That's a good answer."

"Thank you."

"So: What about humility?" The boy was entranced by these ideas and suddenly found himself wanting to understand more.

"Humility is a sense of our smallness in the vast sweep of things, and a recognition of the greatness in other people, along with a realization that we need each other in order to accomplish our best dreams. Absolutely anyone and anything can teach us, as I'm teaching you on this marvelous night."

"I see. This makes sense to me. But it's also strange. I'm big and I'm small."

"Yes. And so are we all. Each of us is of inestimable importance. Yet, none of us owns all the wisdom and virtue of the world. You need others. And they need you. Humility recognizes our wonderful limits. Nobility embraces what is also ours and is limitless." This was a lot for Walid to take in all at once. But he could feel that these words resonated with truth.

The old man continued. "Humility means being open to learn from everyone and everything that crosses our path. The camel can teach us. The storm can teach us. The viper can teach us. Our mistakes can teach us. The stars can, too. If you're humbly open to learning and growing, then you can become everything you're meant to be, in the fullness of your inner nobility. In addition, a proper humility allows you to serve others eagerly and well, and there is nothing nobler than that."

"So, nobility and humility go together."

"They're meant to walk arm-in-arm. But, unfortunately, each of these qualities often wanders along without its intended mate. When they work together, there's magic, and there's tremendous power for good. Combined, they lead to extraordinary things."

This was important for the boy to grasp well. The old man thought for a moment, and then continued. "The greatest kings and leaders on earth are both noble and humble. One who is noble and not humble is presumptuous and arrogant. One who is humble and not noble is hesitant and lost, and never in possession of his full power. To be the great regent you're here to become, you must embrace both these qualities, my friend. Nobility and humility together form the path of true greatness."

The old man paused for a moment. "Nobility and humility are also a part of the oasis within each of us."

"What do you mean?" Walid was clearly concentrating on each word.

Ali smiled. "When you feel appropriate nobility and humility, you're big enough, and strong enough not to be threatened by those things in the world that could otherwise cause you stress and anxiety. Your sense of self is healthy and robust. You're refreshed and protected by what you know, and what you feel."

"That makes a lot of sense," the boy replied.

The old man nodded his head. And he knew there was one more aspect of this lesson that he wanted to pass along. So he said, "It's the often forgotten job of political kings and queens in our world, along with princes and princesses, to model these qualities—nobility and humility. In fact, it's their task to do this so well that they work themselves out of a job."

"What do you mean, Uncle?"

"Ultimately, the one original and legitimate purpose of political royalty has been to provide a source and continuity of governance for people who may not yet be ready to take on that task and rule themselves, while preparing them for precisely that. The end goal, and the enduring purpose, of such royalty is simply to be symbolic—to represent the royalty of the spirit that every man and woman should embody, blending service and significance. The worldly, political phase of monarchy was always meant to be temporary, but it became a thing unto itself, grasped and exploited rather than being used for the good of all. That is a corruption and a perversion, twisted into something harmful."

"I see. That's too bad."

"Yes. We must live to see this reversed. The long winter of distortion in which so many nations, across the globe, have lived must one day give rise to a spring time of new attitudes and actions, when people will rule themselves well and responsibly, reflecting both the noble and humble aspects of the human condition. And it's great individuals like you, my boy, who can lead the way." The old man smiled.

Walid was back in their tent now, sitting on his blanket. He remained quiet for a few moments. His thoughts drifted back over what his great teacher had been saying.

"Uncle, you're clearly exaggerating for dramatic effect who I am and what I can do."

"I assure you, my friend, there's no way to exaggerate the importance of who you are and the extent of what you can do, if you choose to harness the awesome resources of the royal spirit within you, and allow yourself to grow appropriately into the full range of your power. There are no sure limits to the good you can do, and to the number of people you can affect. More is possible than you can even begin to imagine right now."

"No one has ever told me that."

"Remember what I said earlier, that there are things yet to be revealed."

"I thought you were kidding."

"I do like to joke and kid around, but always in service to

truth. Nothing is ever really funny unless it touches on something true. That's why we can often follow small glimmers of humor to important new discoveries and, occasionally, deep realizations. Even a poor joke can sometimes convey a rich insight."

There were a few more moments of silence between them that seemed just right.

"Why do you think I'm so special?"

"Because you are, young man. We're all born special, with a birthright to greatness. But only those who understand this and choose to live the royal path will ever sense the full nature of their potential destiny. Far too many people fail to ascend to their appointed thrones, and by their thoughts, attitudes, and actions choose to exile themselves from the great portion in life that was to be theirs. But you, my boy, are one who is already well along in the process of ascending."

"This is big stuff, Uncle."

"As big as the sky on a night like this."

"It's going to be hard for me to get to sleep after hearing these things."

"Even a prince and future king must sleep."

"I suppose so." Walid smiled.

Ali said, "The kingdom will await your awakening, I assure you. And tomorrow, we may discuss this more. But, for now, the inner needs of true sovereignty beckon us to drowse, and then to dream. Afterwards, we can follow our best dreams, as we may."

The boy stretched his arms wide and yawned. "In that case, I should bid you a royal good night."

"And a wonderful evening of repose to you, Your Highness."

They both smiled in the warm and pleasant darkness, and somehow knew that very good things were soon to come.

7

ANOTHER NEW DAY

A NEW DAY CAN BEGIN LONG BEFORE THE SUN KNOWS WHAT'S GOING ON.

The old man awoke, as always, before dawn. He stretched out his arms and legs, calling on muscles and tendons that had already done a lifetime of work, and inwardly greeted the day before it was quite ready to return his acknowledgment.

And yet, within a few minutes, the early morning chose to smile kindly on him. The smells of breakfast cooking nearby entered the tent and woke the boy, while silently reassuring Ali that he was still invited to partake in many delights of the world, despite his advancing age. He knew well the inner joys that had been produced primarily by living fully every day of that age, and he relished them all. But the simple bodily pleasure of a good breakfast was not to be minimized.

Walid yawned softly and Ali whispered, "Are you awake, my boy?"

"Yes, Uncle. Either that, or else I'm dreaming that I smell food."

The old man laughed. "That would be a most pleasant dream. But I believe we're both awake. So, let's go and have something to eat."

Walid smiled. He said, "You always have good ideas."

"I thank you. But not all lead to such immediate results as we can clearly anticipate this morning."

They pulled on their sandals and then a short walk from the tent brought them into view of a small flame and glowing embers, surrounded by several shadowy figures. They could now begin to hear the sounds of muffled conversations around the fire. And at that moment, with a light gust of breeze, they were caught up even more fully into the wonderful aromas that grew stronger as they drew near.

"Ali! Walid! Please join us for some food." One of the men at the fire called out this greeting and began gathering things for them. When they had come close, he handed them bowls of something good and warm, and then two cups steaming with dark hot tea.

The old man smiled. "Thank you. We can now rouse our bodies with delicious food and drink, and our minds with lively conversation."

Their impromptu chef and waiter replied, "Yes! Come, then! Sit with the morning repast, and right away join in the talk!"

The old man and the boy settled down onto the sand with the others, as their good friend explained, "We were just conferring about the day's journey ahead of us. We'll be passing a place where bandits often come, as you know. The topic was brought up by one of our newer drivers." There were several nods around the fire.

Ali took a sip of tea and commented. "Yes, we've all heard of those men. They come along now and then. We're more numerous than they, and we're well prepared. No camel train of our size has ever been set upon by such criminals. It's too great a risk for them."

A younger man spoke. "Nevertheless, I would imagine that, in your wisdom, you would likely be the first to remind us that we should be on guard and proceed with caution."

The old man turned to him. "Certainly, my brother, and I thank you for your kind words. But I do have strong hopes and a reasonable expectation of peaceful travel today, without conflict or trouble."

"May you be right, my friend, as is your custom." The man seemed to force a smile, or so it appeared to Walid, and then he looked down.

Ali nodded his head in an appreciative way. Then he said, to the men nearest around him, as well as to his nephew, "You know, people often ask of a place whether it's safe or dangerous, as if it has to be either one or the other. And yet, the truth is often more subtle than this. The place up ahead that we'll be passing today indeed has a reputation. But the real truth about it is more complex than the reports and gossip of travelers would lead us to believe."

There were some murmurs of agreement around the fire, and he went on. "It's often that way in life. We tend to think in polarities, or opposites—up or down, left or right, near or far, on or off, dead or alive, good or evil, safe or dangerous. And sometimes, reality is as simple as those thoughts. But at other times, it's more complicated. We often suppose ourselves to be confronted with such opposites, or at least deeply divergent possibilities, and we feel forced to choose—What will it be: This or that, here or there? And yet, the contraries and apparent antitheses in life are often merely partial reflections of greater unities that are instead what we need to understand."

Another of the men said, "Ali, that's deep and insightful."

Then, Walid spoke up from curiosity. "Uncle, if I could ask a simple question, there's something that puzzles me. Why are there bandits in the desert at all?" The boy scraped up some of the food in his bowl as he posed his question. "Why don't they stay in a town or a city where there are many more people to rob?"

"They're not looking for many, my boy, but for a few. Many could resist and overcome them. But out here, a lone traveler or a hapless pair of adventurers, even a small group, would be no match for them. They like solitary places where they can feel more powerful. In the desert, they're hoping that no one else can observe their misdeeds and put an end to their ways."

"But, you really believe they won't come and try to rob us?"

"It's unlikely, if they have any sense at all. We are many. They are few. And we have Masoon, here, our morning chef, waiter, and, I might add, human viper, if I may say so with complete kindness and great respect, but only a viper of the very nicest sort, who would never strike his friends."

The man being referred to in such a way laughed aloud and repeated the word, "Never!"

Ali smiled and continued, "Yet, anyone who attacks him had better be well thought of in heaven, for he can dispatch an assailant to that destination, or to an appropriate alternative, in an instant. He's known far and wide for his great ferocity in defense of his friends."

Masoon laughed again and said, "I'd much rather just cook and serve the food here than skewer a few ragged bandits. But you're correct, Ali, in your assurance that I'll always defend my friends." He lifted his cup in salute to the old man and the boy and gestured to the others around the fire.

He then continued, "I'll most likely have nothing to do at all on this fine day to protect us. And neither will you." He looked at a few of the others and said, "Ali is right. The place we'll pass through is not in itself either dangerous or safe. The fact is that truth blows on the wind here in the desert. The word is out that I travel with this group, and that it includes many strong and fearsome men. Because of this, the thoughts in the minds of the bandits will alone chase them off and keep them far from us."

The old man nodded in agreement. "Walid and I reflected last night on the power of thought. It's actually something we speak of often, now that he's attained the advanced and important age of thirteen."

Masoon laughed and answered, "That's very good." He looked at Walid and said, "True strength begins with our thoughts. True weakness does, too. Most battles in life are won or lost in the realm of thought, before any physical activity takes place. Great things are accomplished by great thoughts."

Ali replied, "Indeed. What you say is wise. My nephew is

already showing that he understands well the inner kingdom of thought. I'm trying to be of help to him in that regard on this journey, his first caravan across the desert, as you know. We're having many chances on these days of travel to talk about the deeper things of life."

Walid then spoke up. "Uncle Ali began sharing his thoughts with me back at the oasis. And he's continued the lessons ever since."

"What have you been discussing with your uncle?" Masoon set down his cup, spread his feet wider apart, and leaned forward with keen anticipation.

"Well, for one thing, I loved our visit to the oasis and didn't want to leave. Uncle Ali could tell."

"Yes. I noticed you were having fun with the boys from the other caravan," Masoon said.

"It was great. I enjoyed it so much that I could have stayed for a long time. I really wanted to. But then Uncle explained to me that I have the power to take an oasis with me wherever I go, in my mind and in my heart. The rest, refreshment, and good feeling that's to be found there can be created within, as I learn to live in the present moment, have peace inside me, and take the right attitude toward difficulties and troubles, whenever they might come. It's all about having what he called the right perspective." The boy spoke with a measure of understanding that might be thought beyond his years. He couldn't hide the hint of a smile as he realized this, and an unexpected feeling of pride warmed his face.

The old man smiled, too. "You can see how good a student he is."

The other men nodded and voiced approval, and the boy continued. "Then Uncle taught me about balance in life, about how we're always a little out of balance, but that, if we're properly self-aware, we can move to rebalance and adjust continually as we go along in our journeys. We work, we play, we rest, and then we work some more. We're sometimes with friends, and sometimes with family. This is true balance. Uncle calls it the dance of life."

Masoon laughed. "I didn't know you still dance, Ali!"

The old man had a slight chuckle in his voice. "Not often, and yet, now and then, perhaps a little jig or a few simple steps. But I can talk of dance at any time."

"Yes, and I can talk of love and pretty women!" Masoon laughed and slapped himself on the knee.

At that, several of the men laughed loudly and others chuckled and shook their heads. The boy grinned with a touch of embarrassment and looked down at the fire.

"Tell me more of your new philosophy," Masoon said as he looked back at the boy.

Walid gathered his thoughts. "Well, on the morning of the storm, I thought it would be a beautiful day and an easy journey because we had such a pleasant start. Uncle Ali didn't rush so quickly to a conclusion about the whole day. He enjoyed the morning, like I did, but he told me that we would deal with whatever the day might bring our way. It was almost as if he knew things would change."

Masoon replied, "Things often do change. We should be most surprised when they don't. And that was quite a storm."

"It was my first time in such a tempest, as Uncle referred to it. I have to admit that I was afraid, but he was calm and strong. He told me what to do, and to do it quickly. Afterwards, I was ashamed that I had been so full of certainty, announcing with confidence that it would be such a fine day. But even about that, he taught me a lesson. He said that, indeed, it was a good day to still be alive!"

"Yes. Your uncle is a very wise man." Masoon chuckled but spoke with conviction. Then he added, "We're all greatly blessed to know him. He helps every one of us to deal with the storms of life."

Ali smiled and nodded his appreciation, and then took up the story, saying, "I thank you, my friend. Right before the worst of the wind fully hit, at the very outset of the tempest, as the great power pounded us and the sand tore at our skin, I could see that Walid was worried about how we could protect ourselves from such violence. I told him that we simply use what we have, which seems to be a general truth and necessary procedure in life. If we keep our wits about us, we can deal with almost any situation."

"I remember how you said it," Walid commented. "Your words have stayed with me. You said: We use what we have. We stay calm. And we move quickly."

"Yes, that's right," Ali smiled.

Walid looked at Masoon and a couple of the other men, and added, "I gained some important lessons that day. We can learn from anything, even a frightening storm. But we have to pay attention and use our minds well. I'll always remember what Uncle Ali told me at the end of the storm. He said: 'We can't control the day, but only what we make of the day. And we'll always make the best of whatever comes our way.' I like that way of looking at life."

Masoon nodded vigorously. "Very good. Very good. That's the attitude to take with you through everything. Don't worry about what you can't control. Focus on what you can control. And then, make the best of it. The power we have over our thoughts and actions is great power, indeed." He reached for his cup, took a swig of the strong, dark tea, and set it back down, wiping his mouth with his large hand.

"It's so true," another man said, and several others voiced their agreement as well, with various comments around the fire.

Masoon smiled and nodded and then addressed the boy again. He said, "I heard that you saw that dangerous snake shortly after the storm. What did you make of it?"

"Yes, the snake! Well, he wasn't that dangerous when I saw him—he was dead! But what a thing to see! Uncle spoke to me that day about harmless snakes and deadly ones, and about many other things that can help us or hurt us. He talked about the two powers, for good and for ill, and how it's often up to us whether help or harm results from an object, or a situation. We should always be on guard to use things well and do our best in every circumstance."

The boy looked at Masoon for a moment in silence and suddenly laughed. "I never thought I'd be glad to be in the company of a live viper, and to talk to one up close!"

They all chuckled at the boy's boldness in using these words. He had spirit, they could see. And this was a very good sign for his future.

Walid paused for a moment, as if embarrassed that he had been so forward as to joke this way with the much older and respected Masoon. But the great warrior just smiled again, looked around at all their companions, and nodded at the boy with kindness.

The old man then carried on the narrative of more recent conversations with a measure of appropriate pride in his voice.

"Last night, we talked about the inner royalty of the mind, the kingdom within us, and how we can properly extend its borders, even perhaps without limit. We also spoke of political monarchy and its true nature."

Ali was glad to be able to share this with men who understood. Words of hearty affirmation among them indicated how impressed they were that the boy was already hearing of such deep and important matters.

Walid piped in immediately. "Uncle told me about things I had never heard of before. He talked about true greatness, and nobility, and humility, and kings, and power. It was all so good and surprising, and interesting. Why don't people speak of it more—in fact, all the time?"

The words, "Yes, yes," and "Indeed," could be heard from several of the men.

Ali sighed and answered the boy with a serious and almost sad look on his face. He said, "Most people don't speak of these things because they don't understand them. They won't even hear of them. They think that these vital perspectives on life are simply foolishness and nonsense."

"But why?" Walid asked.

"Too many people won't open their minds and hearts to

the wonders that belong to them. It's as if they're afraid. They prefer what they already know. And what they know is so little. They allow no room for the miracles that a full embrace of life could bring."

Masoon spoke up. He said, "Yes. A great many people fear their own inner power, as soon as they begin to suspect it. It's far too much responsibility, and because of that, they turn away from it and deny it so completely that they actually begin to lose their hold on its possibility. Soon enough, they forget they ever glimpsed their real nature. And then, these true and powerful ideas become to them as if they never were. In the end, all those who have run from such great realizations then shrink away to the terrible smallness of the sadly restricted thoughts and lives they have chosen instead."

Masoon seemed to know exactly what the old man and the boy had spoken about in the quiet and stillness of the night.

After a few moments of silence, the youngest among them broke the spell. "You can be sure that I'll be one who claims my birthright as a prince of the spirit and then a king! I'll live these things and teach them to others, as I've now been taught."

The boy spoke with pride and a measure of bravado, but also in a seeming spirit of jest, as if testing the men, to see if his words would be accepted as they were genuinely intended. He need not have been concerned.

"Well then, we welcome you into the royal community, the true fellowship of the mind!" Masoon announced heartily, and they all clapped their hands or slapped their knees, while making many other sounds of friendly acclamation. "To the prince and future king!" He lifted his cup high.

"To the prince and future king!" The others repeated the toast and laughed warmly, with obvious gladness, and in that special friendship of the heart that's always happy to see another person ascend properly toward their own best future, and join the ranks of those who live most fully.

The boy had the biggest smile on his face that he had ever experienced. And the old man felt a surge of joy in his heart.

It would be a good new day, indeed.

And much was yet to be revealed.

8

A WISDOM BUCKET

SOME IDEAS CAN RECONFIGURE THE WAY WE THINK AND ACT.

Walid was spinning a small wooden top on a dark blue book lying flat in the sand. He stopped for a moment and gazed over at the old man, who was sitting across from him, reading. "Uncle, I have a question."

Ali replied, "Good. I have many answers. One may fit your needs."

The boy laughed and said, "Ok, here's the question, and I hope it doesn't come out wrong. But, why does everyone look up to you so much? They all treat you like you're really special, and different. I mean, you're certainly very special to me, but everyone else seems to feel the same way. And you're not everybody's uncle."

At that, Ali laughed.

"I heard Masoon say that you're the wisest person he's ever met."

The old man put down his book and smiled. "He's kind."

"Yes, but it's everyone else, too. They all see you as unusually wise and insightful."

"They do me honor."

"Because of who you are, and what you do."

"I thank you." He paused for a moment and said, "I think it may be simply because I have what seems to be a rare cluster of habits."

"What are they?"

"I watch people, like you do, and I think a lot about what I see. I pay attention to nature as it shows itself around us. And I try to draw lessons from the experiences I've had. I ask questions, like you're doing now. I read good books, and I often read them more than once. Then, I think about what they've shown me, or told me. I test their ideas." He pointed to the book the boy had just used as a base for his twirling top. "I've read that one, carefully, three times."

Walid picked up the top and held it in his hand, staring at the book on which it had been spinning. "Is that how you become wise?"

The old man took a deep breath and exhaled slowly. "That's a good part of what it takes to become wise. But I must tell you, my good friend, an important part of it, I don't fully understand."

"What do you not understand—you, of all people, who understand so much?"

Ali looked off into the distance for a moment, and then said, "I'm not sure how to put this into words. But I'll try." He stroked his beard, and went on, "Every now and then, something like a hole in the sky opens up, a special place that we can't see, and thoughts fall down through it from heaven like a beautiful rain of good feeling and deep insight. I don't know how this happens, or when it will take place. But I always have a bucket ready to catch these waters of wisdom as they come."

The boy smiled. "What do you mean? Where's your bucket?"

"My wisdom bucket is in my heart."

"Oh. Ok. I see. I think. So, how can I have a bucket, too?"

"It's good that you ask. Most people never do. Those who ask this question show by the asking that they already have such a container in place." The old man nodded slightly and continued to speak.

"You, my boy, are blessed with a fine bucket for wisdom, and I would venture to suggest it will be ready at all times for any insight that may fall down to you from above." He held his large, rough hands out as if he were holding on to the sides of such a recepticle.

"How will I know this is happening? How can I recognize when it's raining these waters of wisdom that I should capture and keep?"

Ali said, "That's easy. You may be talking with someone, or reading, or sitting alone. You could be walking in an isolated place, or be in the midst of a crowd. It can happen at any time, even when you're asleep, in a dream, or in your first thoughts, as you wake. You'll feel something good pour into your heart. You'll experience insights, ideas, and new perspectives that you've never had before. These revelations might solve a problem that you've been confronting. Or they may point the way forward along a new path. They could clear up a mystery, or help you to a new realization. When they come, grab hold quickly, think on them, ponder them, and even write them down to help commit them to memory."

Walid replied, "I started keeping an idea diary when we were in the oasis. I record the insights I get from our talks, and other thoughts."

"Excellent! I've seen you writing at night, and at other times. I'm glad this is why. You have good instincts for what to do."

"I've been recording things you say, and then other things that just come to me out of the blue and bring me a feeling of understanding."

Ali nodded and said, "Good. You see, this is what I mean. When special insight comes, this rain from above, you'll feel connected to something important and ancient and wise. It's both outside you and yet somehow also inside you at the same time. As you feel this, and make yourself open to the new thoughts, keeping them in your heart and mind, your wisdom bucket will be filled. And other people will come to you for a drink."

"They come to you all the time."

"Yes, they do. And I'm glad."

"I've never seen you refuse anyone. You always make time and give people what they need."

"I do so freely. It's my joy to give."

"I think that's very good. But I can imagine somebody else wondering why you don't keep your wisdom to yourself, for just your own use."

"Oh, my boy, this is crucial. Wisdom is for everyone. Those

who don't understand that don't yet have it. They may say the right words, but true wisdom isn't in their hearts unless they deeply desire both to live it and share it. Wisdom is for keeping and using and also for giving away. It's not for hoarding. Remember the man who piled up his treasure. It's good to use and share what we have. In fact, it's often in the act of passing along wisdom that we come to grasp and appreciate it even more deeply. We thereby become wiser."

"I think I understand that. I like what you're saying."

"Heaven may have opened a hole in the sky for you just now, my boy. And I think you're already using your wisdom bucket to collect the insight. This means that, soon, you can share it with others."

"I really want to do that. And you're showing me how."

"Good. If you desire anything deeply enough, then that desire itself is a key to its own fulfillment."

Walid said, "Why is that?"

Ali replied, "Our deepest desires come to us as signs of who we are and what we can do. If you want something with all your heart, from the deepest place inside you, backed up by all your most cherished beliefs and your highest values, and the aspiration will not leave you, then you can be assured that this desire is leading you along a path you need to walk."

"I do want to have wisdom like you, Uncle, and to share it as you do, with anyone who needs it. Right now, that's my deepest desire."

"I can tell that you mean what you say, my boy. Be of strong hope and good faith. I believe that great things are meant for you, as you receive, live, and share wisdom. There's greatness in your future."

Walid thought for a second. "A lady said something like that to me back at the oasis."

"Is that right?"

"Yes. I didn't tell you about it then because I was a little embarrassed, and it was all a bit strange. But, one afternoon while we were there, an older lady called me to come over to her. She was sitting under a shady tree and had seen me playing ball with some of the other boys. I walked over to where she sat. She asked to see my hands."

"She did?"

"Yes. I showed her, and she looked closely at them and then at me. She gazed right into my eyes and said, 'Great things are meant for you. I see something golden in your future, young man.' Then she smiled at me and said, 'I don't mean to be mysterious, but I had a strong feeling about you just a moment ago, and I needed to see you up close and tell you. Now, you can return to your play. Be deeply blessed in all ways.' And that's all she said. I thanked her for her kind words, then went back to kicking the ball with the other boys."

Ali nodded and said, "She was right. I know the lady you mean. She's a person with a powerful gift of insight. I didn't realize you had met her. Her words will come true. You will indeed do many great things in your life. The wisdom you gather now will help to assure it."

"Thank you, Uncle, for saying that, and for sharing all this with me." The boy looked down at the book lying in the sand at his feet.

"Does this book contain and share wisdom that I could gather?"

"Yes it does. You can tell as you read that the man who

wrote it had long filled his own bucket with that special rain from above."

Walid picked the worn and much used volume up off the sand and looked at it more closely. "Are most books like that?"

"Sadly, the answer to your question is no. Many books are written from research and study, from the top of the head, but not the bottom of the heart. And others spring from a vivid imagination, but not many come from the deepest sources of wisdom. Those poor authors pour no real inspiration onto their pages, largely because they've not collected any themselves, in the way we're discussing.

"A great many books contain information, or entertainment, or provide readers with an experience that can be gripping, and yet without true enlightenment. Their words have no special spark of wisdom. But when real wisdom is in the writer's heart, it pours forth across the pages, carried by the words that appear there, and it leaps out for people like you and me to discover and cherish and use, and then share with others. As we read, the insight falls like rain into our hearts, and we can feel it, and we know we need to use our buckets quickly to catch it. But we can't often capture it all the first time. That's why we read a very good book again, and perhaps again. We go back for more of the refreshing nourishment and growth it can bring."

Walid was absorbing all of these thoughts. He had to ask: "Do you normally read a book more than one time?"

"Yes, indeed, if it's a good one. If a book's not worth reading twice, it wasn't worth reading once. Any book created from a wellspring of wisdom will contain more than you can experience and capture on your first encounter with it. You have to ponder it and read it again, and savor it like a tasty fruit full of juice, and then perhaps discuss with others what you've learned. That way, your bucket grows full."

The boy asked, "Does everyone feel this rain from heaven, these insights that pour into the heart?"

Ali answered, "At some time or another, I believe they do. But to continue to experience this, you have to remain open and eager for the insights to come. You need to pay attention, and listen with your heart. Many people busy themselves so much, they never have time to fully listen and feel the beautiful cool rain of insight that can be theirs."

The boy repeated the point to make sure he understood, because it sounded so strange to him. "People are too busy to feel the special rain of insight that pours down from heaven?"

"That's right. Have you ever seen an umbrella?"

"Yes, in our village, but only a few times, and the ones I saw were carried by visitors. I've also seen them in pictures—several ladies and a few men holding them, either to provide shade from the sun, or to protect their clothing from rain."

"The people who stay too busy all the time, their constant busyness forms a big umbrella that can keep any drops of inspiration, or even downpours of insight, from reaching them. It's sad."

"But other people do feel this rain of wisdom?"

"Yes, and yet, too many of them have no bucket for catching the insight they receive. They don't truly take it in. And others have only an old bucket full of holes. They capture the new thoughts for a while, but then the bucket leaks, and they've lost the wisdom they had captured for all too brief a time. After this, when life deals them a difficult challenge or an unusual opportunity and they need the insight, it's gone and no longer available for them to use."

Walid said, "I guess then that I need to keep my wisdom bucket ready all the time, and make sure it has no holes or leaks that would allow the insights I catch to be lost."

Ali smiled. "The best way to avoid a leaky bucket is to love wisdom in your heart, seek it everywhere, meditate on what you learn, use it all that you can, and be ready at any time to share it freely. That will keep your bucket in good repair."

He continued, "Wisdom is in some ways like other things. The more we seek it, the more of it we find. And in other ways it's different from most things. The more we use what we have, the deeper, richer, stronger, and more expansive it gets. The more we give it away, the more firmly we retain it, and it also then grows. And here is perhaps the deepest of insights: Wisdom is not just about words, but actions. It's an embodied art, a skilled behavior, a way of living. It's about the greatest insights percolating down into habits, dispositions, and inclinations of thinking, feeling, and doing that will guide your path in life. As we fill our bucket, and use what it contains, it gets bigger and able to hold more, which is both strange and wonderful."

"This is so interesting, Uncle. I'll seek to keep my bucket in good repair. I'll use it. And I'll freely share with others from it."

"Very good, my boy. Keep your bucket always available and in good shape."

At that very moment, the camel standing near them kicked his water bucket, snorting loudly, and they both laughed.

9

THE FOUR ELEMENTS

IT WAS TWILIGHT.

The heat of the day had gone its way, trailing the sun off to the west and leaving a pleasant, light breeze to sweep away its memory. The travel of the day was over. The additional coolness of the evening was just beginning to be felt. Tents had been pitched, and after a quick dinner, the men of the caravan were preparing in their various ways for the morning that would next rouse them from sleep and invite them once more to their trek across the sand. Camels were tended, equipment was checked, and the things from their meal, like pots and bowls, were cleaned and put away.

The old man had been talking with Masoon and a few of the other camel drivers, sitting in a small circle that was thirty or forty feet from the tent he shared with his nephew. The conversation was low, and it seemed serious. After about ten minutes, the men got up, nodded or gestured toward Ali, and walked back to their own tents, while the old man returned to his. Walid had been watching from a distance. He knew that the men often conferred about travel or supplies, but this was a much smaller group than usual, and the men had seemed to show expressions of great concentration as they talked.

Ali walked up to where the boy was sitting, and before Walid could express his curiosity over what the meeting was about, his uncle gave him a look of quizzical concern and stopped and said, "Do you know how to swim, my boy?" It was an odd question to ask in the middle of the desert, far from any bodies of water, but the old man clearly had something on his mind.

"No, Uncle, I don't. But I've certainly heard about it, and one time I saw some people, at a distance, swimming in a river."

"We'll come to a place soon, another oasis, with a small pond of water that's good for swimming. If you'd like, I'll show you how."

"Great! I loved the little pool at our first oasis. I sat at the edge of it on some stones and put my feet in the water. It felt cool and nice."

Ali smiled and nodded his head. Then he asked, "Do you understand the true importance of water?"

Walid replied, "I know we need it to drink, and so do the camels, but not as often."

"Yes. We can go for a long time without food, but only a short time without water. It's necessary for our lives."

"I've never really thought about that."

"The men and I were just talking about our water supply, and some other important matters, and our discussion set my mind off in a certain direction. I'll give you an important lesson this evening, if you're ready to learn something fundamental about life."

"Yes, I am, please. I'm glad we've stopped for the nightly rest. But I don't feel like sleep any time soon. I'd love for you to teach me something first. I'm ready to hear whatever you'd like to share."

The old man bent over and brushed at the sand next to Walid. He then sat down near the boy, thought for a moment, and lit a small lantern that was on the ground within reach. Satisfied with its placement and the light it was providing, he now smoothed the sand in front of them with the side of his hand, as he said, "Let me prepare something here." Then he drew in the level sand, with a single finger, a simple square, with one line bisecting it horizontally, and another crossing in the center at a right angle, resulting in four small boxes. He pursed his lips slightly, and spoke.

"The ancients believed that there are four elements out of which everything in our world is made, and from which everything happens. They are earth, air, water, and fire." He pointed to each of the squares as he spoke these four names, then pointed back at one of them and made a mark.

"Earth is clearly of great importance. We walk on the earth and we eat its bounty. Like all life, we're creatures of the earth, and one day our bodies will return to it. Meanwhile, it provides us with our shelter as well as with food, and with all the materials from which we make everything we have. The earth is often even said to be our mother."

"I've heard that expression." The boy was paying close attention.

Ali continued, now pointing to a second square and marking it. "The air, of course, is what we breathe. Without it, we couldn't live. On the inside, it allows our bodies to function. On the outside, this same air also makes it possible for us to see and signal, and hear and speak. By its conveyance, we can smell someone cooking our food long before we see the meal."

"Yeah, really," Walid said, "I remember how much we enjoyed the aroma of breakfast the other day, as soon as we left the tent."

"Indeed."

"It woke us up and welcomed us to the group around the fire, where we had our food and morning talk. The smell was so good!"

The old man smiled at the memory. He said, "Yes. That day, the aromas were floating directly to our tent. And, think about it. What comes to us through the air can welcome us, or it can warn us. The air is a messenger of many things. It carries the birds, and far too often, out here, the sand. The wind, a brisk movement of air, at our backs can ease our journey, or in our faces, can slow our progress. It can cool us as a breeze, or it can bring us big storms."

Walid replied, "I guess that's another example of the two powers."

"It is. When I was a boy like you, an old man in my town would joke with me and my friends and ask us riddles like this one:

> 'What's now, will be, and long has been
> Around us everywhere, yet can't be seen?
> You can touch it too, whenever you please,
> But it's truly something you never can seize!'

"I remember that to this one, two of us right away said, 'God!' and he laughed, and in a funny, dramatic voice augmented with gestures, he replied, 'You boys are profound! Your insights abound! But perhaps it's something else you can't see. Shh! Just between you and me: It's here and it's there —it's … ordinary air.'"

"That's funny, Uncle."

"You must understand, he was a man who often spoke with a riddle, rhyme, or even a joke."

"Ha! You did it just now!"

"You're a good listener, and clever."

"Thank you. I try."

"So, I imagine that you fully understand the importance of earth and air, the first two elements?"

"Yes, I think I do. And I know the importance of water. We drink it, and wash in it, and we splash it on our faces!" Walid was clearly enjoying these thoughts. His engagement in the ideas lifted his voice. "Also, we can swim in it!" He added this with a triumphant smile and an imitative movement of his arms.

"Yes, you're right. Plus, its importance goes much farther. The plants, animals, and people of our world couldn't live at all without water. It's the true elixir of life. We irrigate with it, we refresh ourselves by it, we cleanse ourselves in it, and we cook using it. We can even move great distances because of its quality and quantity, transporting explorers and armies and teachers and goods in boats and ships on rivers and seas around the world."

"I've seen boats in pictures, but I've never seen one in person, or been on one." Walid inwardly remembered his surprise the first time he saw a photograph of a river with two boats gliding down it. "I'd love to see the ocean at some point, and one of the big ships I've read about that travel on it! That would be great." With these words, he fell silent for a moment, in thought. And then Ali spoke again.

"One day, you will see the ocean, the largest body of water. And it will speak to you in its own voice. It will whisper to you of adventure and possibility and beauty and treasure beyond imagining. It will lure you and perhaps even frighten you a little with its immensity. But you'll feel an affinity, or connection, with it that you won't fully comprehend."

Walid said, "Why is there a special connection?"

Ali replied, "The ocean is made of salt water, and much of your body is the same."

"It is?"

"Yes, despite all surface appearances to the contrary."

"I didn't know that."

"It has consequences. Like speaks to like. And then, there's more. The seemingly limitless horizon of the sea, smooth and apparently perfect, naturally represents for us the infinite, symbolizing something deep within us, as well as outside us, something ancient and powerful that encompasses us, something with which we're intimately connected. And so, for this reason also, we resonate with it at the most fundamental level. Some even tell us that all life once came from the sea. It calls to us, and it can inspire all our voyages through this world, even on land and across a vast desert like this."

"I do want to experience all that."

"You will, my boy, you will. The time will come for you."

"But can I ask a question, Uncle? Something's bothering me."

"Ask anything."

"I understand very well the importance of earth, air, and water—these three. But, what of fire? How can it possibly be their equal? We cook our food with it, and warm our bodies on cold nights near it and, like, with this lantern, it helps us to see, but what else does it do? I learned when I was young that fire depends on wood from the earth, and straw and grass, as well as on oxygen from the air. But dirt can smother it. And water can put it out. So how can it be as important as these other three elements?"

"Oh, my boy, here is a deep secret for you. Fire is the most important of them all."

"I don't understand. How can that be?"

"The sun is fire, my boy. The stars are fire. We could not live without the energy of these fires. No life would exist on earth without the power from the sun."

Walid then jumped in with a measure of excitement in his voice and a new spark in his eyes. "We couldn't see at all without the sun."

His uncle nodded and smiled again. "That's true, in two ways. The sun itself brings life to be, and then gives us the light to see."

The eager student wanted to repeat this thought, as he often did to make sure he would remember something. "The sun itself brings life to be, and then gives us the light to see." He paused for a second, and said, with a smile, "Without the fire of the sun and the stars, or the small fires we light, there would be total darkness!"

"That's right, my friend. And you couldn't chase your shadow."

Walid laughed and said, "But then again, I guess I wouldn't be around for it to chase me, either!" Ali laughed, too, enjoying as always his nephew's quick wit and enthusiasm.

They continued and joked a bit more, while the boy made hand puppet shadows from the light of the lantern near them. Then they both grew quiet again and the old man spoke softly.

"The secrets here go even deeper."

"What do you mean?"

"Some say the entire universe began in a gigantic burst of fire, a flaming flash of energy beyond our imagination that spawned everything around us by shooting off dazzling sparks that cooled to make every kind of matter, the building blocks of all physical things. Other sparks were hotter and didn't change in that way."

"What happened to them?"

"They became the stuff of the stars and suns that blaze brightly throughout the cosmic vastness that goes on and on."

"Uncle, that's amazing. How did you learn all this?"

"As you know, I read a lot. And I talk with people who know of such things."

"It stretches my understanding."

"Yes. And in addition to all this, there have been people throughout history who, on one day, or many, have had an unusual experience of the world, a mystical vision of the most fundamental reality beneath all else, where it all suddenly seems ablaze with meaning, and as if to reveal a deeper fire that touches everything around us."

"Wow." Walid paused a moment and thought. Then, he

spoke again. "You told me earlier that some say the earth is our mother. Is fire then something like … our father?"

"Ah. You're asking a good question and coming close to the most ultimate mysteries of all. The fire we know is an image for the deepest of realities. And that is another part of why it's the most important element. But, for now, in this moment, let me continue on, along a facet of all this that you especially need to understand."

"Yes. Please do."

"We have in us the same stuff that structures the universe, the elements found in the stars, and—here's what most people never dream—we have within ourselves the fire."

"How can that be?"

"I can see that you're already warming to the topic, my boy." The old man smiled and reached over and touched Walid's arm. "And you're quite warm to the touch. At all times that you're alive in this physical domain, your body has in it the warmth of energy that comes from the universe. But there's so much more in you, as well."

"What is it? What do you mean?"

"The fire of the spirit, my friend. I see sparks of it in your eyes right now, as I often do."

"Uncle, I see that in your eyes all the time. But I didn't know what to call it."

"Some people say it's a sparkle or a twinkle. Others, that there's a gleam or a flash. But at its core, it's the version of fire within your soul—a spiritual flame, in some ways like its familiar physical counterpart, but on another, and deeper, and yet also higher level of existence."

The boy looked puzzled. "Does everyone have this fire of the spirit inside?"

The old man replied, "I believe that, at birth, we all have it. As babies grow, you can sometimes see it reflected on their faces and, especially, in their eyes. But as the years pass, many things in the world threaten to smother this initially small flame and put it out."

"What do you mean?"

Ali thought for a moment and said, "Some people, as they get older, allow the troubles of life and the harsh actions of others to create damp, cold ground all around the little flame in their hearts, and it can't grow or spread in their souls. Their own thoughts and emotions can then even begin to create something like a thick fog inside that threatens to extinguish the flickering inner light. But, then, other people are different. They feed the small fire with positive energy, and it eventually becomes a larger blaze. The many and varied things of life can then become fuel for their fire—even the troubles and obstacles that fall across their path like dead trees and brush and trash. These things are thrown onto their growing flame, which burns strong enough to consume all such impediments and feed on them and, as a result, their inner fire becomes bigger and stronger yet."

Walid had a mild look of surprise on his face. "The things that crush and stop some people are just fuel for the fire in others?"

"Yes. Remember what I've said many times. It doesn't matter so much what happens to us as how we deal with what happens to us."

"I do remember, Uncle. It's an important insight about life."

"The people who grow strong with the fire of the spirit, they can suffer the same hardships as everyone else, and feel the weight of the obstacles and difficulties that sometimes pile on them in great measure. And at times, it may seem to them that it's all just too much and their inner fire will go out. But, precisely when things are darkest, and the buried flame in their hearts perhaps can't even be felt at all, it then suddenly bursts forth again with a greater intensity drawn from the very things that had threatened it."

"I didn't know that. No one has ever told me these things before."

"It's now your time to learn. And so, when troubles come your way, you need not fear them. They will be just more fuel for the fire."

Walid took this thought into his heart. He spoke softly the words: "I won't fear trouble. I'll say to myself, 'Fuel for the fire!' and just burn more brightly."

Ali smiled. "Good! That's the spirit!"

"What you've said about all this inspires me greatly."

"It has long inspired me, to realize these things. And, my friend, there's even more."

"What is it?"

"You may at some times have heard people speak of being tried by fire, using the image of the flame in a different way."

"Yes, I've heard that said."

"People who speak in this way see the difficulties and tribulations in life as things that can purify us the way a refiner's fire burns impurities from precious metals, removing imperfections that are melted away by being exposed to a hot enough flame. Our toughest circumstances may often seem to turn up the heat on us, but always remember that if we tend the flame that's within us, then there's no heat outside us that can be stronger than it, or the deepest resources we have. We can determine what we do with our circumstances, however searing they might be. We can choose what we become through them."

"That's good to know. It's a great perspective to have."

"Yes. This is what I mean when I say that it doesn't matter so much what happens to us as what we do with what happens to us. When we use everything as fuel, we burn more and more brightly, and our inner fire becomes more powerful, and better able to handle even the most difficult challenges. In all things, the fire of inner passion and a good spirit can burn away obstacles and, like the furnace of the sun, provide the energy to bring life to many great things."

Walid said, "So that's what you do. You grow the flame inside you, and use it to burn away obstacles, and bring great energy to life."

"Yes, my boy, that's what I do. And it's a big reason why people are drawn to me and credit me with wisdom. They're attracted to the warmth of the fire. People often feel the cold touch of disappointment and fear and failure and heartache in their lives and need very badly to be warmed. Those of us who have tended the fire well can provide some of the warmth they need. They feel it in us, and draw near."

Ali continued, "You'll recognize individuals who have cultivated the fire of the spirit well. They're different. They sparkle, they glow." He smiled slightly. "They sometimes even smolder. They have a flame that can be passed to others, as a torch in the darkness. People are attracted to their heat, their light, and their positive energy."

The boy nodded his understanding. "I know several people like that. They can walk into a room and light it up. Others gather around them like they would around a campfire. There's often lots of laughter and good feeling in their presence."

"Yes there is. Men and women carry the fire in sometimes different ways, and yet in many similar ways. People with strong fire are especially attracted to others who also have grown their flame. They know at a deep level that they can do remarkable things together."

The old man paused for a moment, then continued. "Great people have great fire. They walk the earth differently. They move through the air brightly, and with confidence. They can almost walk on water!"

The boy and his uncle both smiled at this image that used all four elements. Ali then stroked his beard and spoke again.

"The great person with intense fire reminds me of a tiger."

"In what way?" Walid asked.

"When I was a boy, much younger than you are now, a tiger was brought into our land to be shown to the king. And I had a chance to catch a glimpse of it briefly."

"I've never seen a real tiger, only pictures."

"It's an impressive beast."

"I can imagine."

"The tiger has always represented to me the person with great fire, using all the elements, and burning bright with the inner flame that allows for great accomplishment."

The old man paused for a moment and then continued. "The tiger walks on the earth and eats its bounty, breathes in the air, drinks of the water around him, and lives from the fire within, that impressive strong power and energy symbolized by his flaming-orange fur and his impressive black stripes, a coloration that seems to allude to flickering sharp tongues of fire and dark, powerful smoke."

"Wow, I never thought of that." Walid was impressed.

Ali then smiled and added, "To be the great man you're meant to be, you must embody in your own heart the spirit of the tiger."

Walid smiled, too, and said, "I like that way of thinking, Uncle."

"Good! And here's where the mystery gets compounded. These people with great fire, when they use it well, can also somehow bring to others the soothing nurture of water, and a breath of fresh air, and can even seem to provide them with new, solid ground on which to walk, as they move forward in life. So again, in the realm of the spirit, as in that of the body, fire is somehow the source and support of all."

The boy sat silently for a moment. "That's a lot to think about. It's a lot to understand."

"Yes it is, my boy. Let it be positive fuel for the fire of your mind."

"You've sparked many new thoughts in me, for sure!"

"That's very good. Continue to warm yourself with them, as the evening chill grows. The sun will rise again tomorrow and shed light on many more things connected with what we've spoken about tonight."

10

WHO WE ARE

THE MORNING WAS A GOOD ONE.

There was something like a vibrancy in the air, almost a tangible intimation of interesting things soon to come. Even the camels seemed to sense it. The men who were up earlier than most had an extra measure of energy in their voices and their actions.

After awakening to the still dark new day, the old man and the boy had their breakfast quickly with a few of the others, packed up, and once more began their travel together across the desert for the morning hours. The sun rose with a special fire on this day, and everyone was ready for the mid-day break when it was called. The tents were pitched for shade, as always, to take the edge off the heat and allow for some rest and recovery before the afternoon travel would commence. By nightfall, they would arrive at a second oasis, and they would then be only two or three days out from the big city where this phase of their journey would end, and new adventures begin.

Walid and Ali now lay in the shade of their tent for the time of rest. The younger of the two propped himself up on one arm.

"Uncle, I've been thinking about the four elements and what you taught me last night."

"Good. I'm glad to hear it. You absorb ideas well."

"Thanks. So: You talked about the fire in everyone and how some people tend the flame and grow it, and others don't."

"Indeed."

"You also said that we contain water, and air, which are necessary for life."

The old man nodded. "Very good. You remember accurately."

"You mentioned that some people call the earth our mother."

"I did."

"So, is there earth in us, too? I can't recall whether you said."

"Yes, there is. All four elements dwell in each of us. They're in our bodies and they are in our hearts. But there's usually one that's dominant in a person's spirit."

"What do you mean?"

The old man now propped himself up also to face the boy, and he explained. "Well, last night we spoke the most about fire. That's my dominant element. I have a burning passion for life. I feel the energy of the fire inside me. It's something I've experienced since I was small."

"And others are drawn to your flame," Walid said. He was extremely proud of how all the men seemed to view his uncle.

"Yes. They are. And this is also Masoon's dominant element. It's often primary in creative people like you, my boy, and in warriors like Masoon. But creators and warriors can sometimes express it very differently."

"And yet, they both have inner passion?" Walid was getting the idea.

"They do. They share that in common, however divergently it might be manifested in their lives. And, of course, there are many types of creative people like you. Some are wonderful makers, with their minds or their hands, and others are great performers. A few do both. Remember the tightrope walker I described to you when we first talked about life balance?"

"I do."

"He was a fire person, a creative individual, and a performer. He was quite dramatic in his presentations, and knew what it took to move a crowd to astonishment and wild applause. But other fire people may do their jobs quietly, as they sit alone writing a book, or stand by themselves to work on a painting. The flame inside can glow and be expressed in many ways. Such is the nature of fire."

"How about earth?"

"Well, our friend Mahmood, the man who is most expert in the health of our camels, and who buys our supplies, he's a man of the earth."

"What are these people like?"

"They're solid. They're dependable. You can count on them. They may not be flashy or stand out from the crowd in obvious ways, but they're always there for you. A person in whom earth dominates often provides good soil for new ideas and projects. You may have a spark of insight, and think of a new thing that should be done. But perhaps, you can't do it

alone. You then may need to bring that idea as a seed to people in whom earth dominates, people who will be fertile soil
for your vision, and who can work reliably to make it grow
and bear fruit. Nothing difficult that requires extended effort
and attention to detail can ever be accomplished without the
involvement of good, solid, productive earth people."

The boy picked up on these ideas quickly. "Mahmood
always tends the camels faithfully whether they're well or sick
or hurt, and he never tires of his work. I've always admired
the care he takes in everything he does. He never overlooks
anything. He catches every problem, and takes care of every
need."

Ali nodded his agreement. "He's firm and solid earth. On
him, you can depend. Many skilled artisans are like that, and
especially master craftsmen. They're absolutely dedicated to
excellent work, whether it's appreciated or not. Likewise, a
great number of the world's best scientists are earth people,
even if their minds are in the stars."

Walid smiled at the image and said, "Then, what of water?
How does it appear in people's spirits as a leading element?"

"In a way that you might expect. Water people flow out
to others and nourish them. They're great supporters and
encouragers. They often provide a high tide that lifts up everyone around them. They're good at working with other people,
and keeping great enterprises afloat, organizing and helping to
bring others together. They provide the current along which
projects and people can remain bouyant and row and sail all
the way to the sometimes faraway harbor of proper success.
Water people are very important in life."

The boy said, "I see. That's amazing." He thought for a moment and added, "You know, our friend Hakeem is a water person."

"Yes, he is." The old man smiled.

Walid went on. "He's encouraging to everyone, and supports all his friends. He came to check on us and help us when the storm buried us in sand."

"He did. That's his way. Water people are often the first to help. They rush out to any need when they see it. They refresh others and support them whenever there is a need, or a drought, or a time of scarcity. Hakeem is a very good example of a water person."

The boy lay back and stared up at the tent pole. He seemed for a few seconds to be pondering all this. "But the element of air, Uncle, it puzzles me. What's an air person? What do they do?"

"Think about it for a moment, my boy. Recall what I said last night. We hear sounds conveyed by the air. We smell aromas that come to us on the air. We see through the air. We speak using air."

The boy glanced at the sand. Then he looked up. "The air brings us awareness of new things. It conveys news. Through it, information travels!"

"That's right, and well said. Air is the prime medium of information, communication, and movement. The air moves as wind, and allows other things to move in it. Even water makes its way through the air as rain. And think of the motion when I pour cool juice from a jug into your cup. It goes from one vessel to the other through the air."

"Well, then, what's an air person like? Is he one who communicates and moves, and somehow allows or helps others to move?"

"That's correct. An air person is a communicator, a connector, and a mover. He's a breeze that blows things our way. An air person brings us information we might not have known. He connects us up with resources we may need. And he often provides that push of wind in our sails that we require to lift and nudge our little boats forward on the rivers of life."

"I like that image. The more time we're in the desert, the more we speak of water."

Ali chuckled. "Yes, you're right."

"But tell me more about the air person."

"Certainly. An air person often moves like the wind, and sometimes just as unpredictably, and with surprise. What he brings us can help us make it all the way to our next destination."

The old man appeared to be lost in thought for a moment, before adding: "Air people can provide fresh life to a project or community or friend. They're good to have around."

He then offered one more thought. "Some air people seem to rise above the rough and tumble of life, unscathed by what happens on the ground. They live and move in their own space. They drift lightly above the turmoil that engulfs so many others, and can at times appear untouched and unsoiled by it. We can often gain a good and useful perspective by just being around them. It's no coincidence that the most calming meditation focuses on the air of our breath."

Walid was silent for a second, in contemplation of this.

And then he asked, "Do we have any air people with us on our journey to market?"

Ali responded, "Yes, but not many."

"Who? Can you give me an example?"

"You know Bashir?"

"The big man. Yes."

A quick smile crossed the old man's face, but his voice was serious. "When he eats too many beans, he's a man of great air. There's such a wind afterwards, you could fly a kite."

They both laughed heartily. The boy looked outside the tent to make sure that Bashir was nowhere near. But, there was a slight wind.

"Uncle, you're very funny. I like it. But I mean, really, who among us is a man of air?"

"There's Bancom, for one."

"Bancom?"

"Yes."

"I love it when he plays one of his musical instruments and sings."

"I do, too. We all do. Now, think. What does he sing about?"

"I often hear him sing about people he knows, and also about what's going on in the world."

"Yes. He's a true man of the air. He's a great connector of people and information. Listen to him and you'll learn many useful things. Sit with him long enough and it will be as if you're transported to faraway places. But what he's doing is actually bringing them to you."

"This is all very new to me. I've never thought like this before."

"I know. And it will be useful for you."

"I can imagine. But can you say more about that?"

"Yes. Of course. It helps a great deal to identify the element that dominates or leads in a person, or the one that may be a bit lacking. Then we can relate to that individual most properly. We'll have more reasonable expectations of him, or her. And then we'll understand better what we see that person do. But I should also add that, sometimes, two of the elements seem to rule equally in a life. Such a spirit may balance, for example, earth and water as guiding elements, or even the surprising combination of fire and water."

Walid picked up on this idea right away, and showed his creative understanding. He said, "The combination of earth and water would be a reliable, solid worker who also encourages others well."

"That's correct." Ali was pleased at his student's words.

The boy then continued. "A fire and water person will attract others to his flame, drawing them in his direction, and then support them and keep them afloat."

"You're right. You have a good grasp of this already."

"Are there people with three balanced elements that equally lead the way in their lives?"

"Very few, I suspect. An example would be a person who like fire is passionate, like air connects people and knowledge, and like water nurtures them."

"How about all four? Are there any people who are equally strong in all four elements?"

Ali laughed and said, "I'm not surprised that you ask. I've never met such a person. They may exist, but I believe it would be extremely rare. Perfection in this particular respect, or such a comprehensive and balanced completeness of any sort, for that matter, is not often to be found in our world."

"I see." Walid was in deep thought about what he was hearing. And then, Ali spoke again.

"Remember, though, that we all have each of the four elements in us, just not with equal strength."

Walid nodded. "One more question about this occurs to me, Uncle. You mention only good things with each type of person. Are there bad things, too? What makes me ask this is that I remember well your talk of the two powers, the power to help and the power to harm."

"You typically do remember well. And the answer to your question is yes. There's possible bad as well as good. And we don't even have to mention Bashir and the beans."

Walid laughed again, and Ali continued, with almost a straight face. "I'm joking, of course, but this is truly important to understand. Fire people can burn us. Water people can drown us. Earth people can slow us and bog us down in deep sand, or mud. Air people can blow things into our lives that we don't actually want or need. Remember again the tempest of sand that threatened us all."

"I do." Walid would never forget that experience. "I also remember Bashir's last big meal—and the stormy night that followed."

The old man chuckled. "Ah, yes. But perhaps we should now leave aside poor Bashir, and the special way that he, too, like Bancom, makes music."

They both laughed again.

The old man turned a bit more serious and reflective as he

spoke. "Each of the elements can bring us great good. Each can bring harm. It's up to us, as we find that one or another of these elements may dominate in our personalities, to govern them for good and prevent them from bringing ill to others, as well as into our own lives. A person's greatest strength is most often somehow also the source of his greatest weakness. Every path of delight can be a road to destruction if it's not traveled properly."

"I see."

"I can also put the most general insight related to this in another way, as my old neighbor might have, when I was a boy: There's no good tool in the hand of a fool."

Walid smiled. "That was your neighbor who often rhymed and spoke in riddles."

"Yes. And as we know, a rhyme or a riddle can help us remember an important thought."

Walid repeated the rhyme. "There's no good tool in the hand of a fool." He then thought for a second and said, "I think this means that a foolish man will use anything badly. Nothing he has, no gift or talent or achievement, however impressive it seems, will be beneficial, either to him or to others, if he's truly foolish in how he lives."

"You are knowing beyond your years, my boy. We must take care always to be wise as we develop who we are and what we most naturally do. Your specific nature is a gift to you. Your dominant element or set of leading elements is a powerful resource. But you must use that gift well in order to be a blessing and not a curse in the world, to others and yourself. Used skillfully, your most elemental gift, the most fundamental orientation of your spirit, is the greatest of tools, and can help you to build a life worth living."

"I can then be a blessing, and not a curse."

"That's right—always a blessing, and never a curse. And now, perhaps as a blessing to ourselves, we should nap. We have more hours of journey on the sand ahead of us today."

"Thanks, Uncle. I'll now let a fifth element govern me."

"What's that?"

"Sleep."

"Good boy. Let it arise within you to predominate for a while. We can talk more of these things later."

II

BAD TROUBLE

IT WAS AN HOUR AFTER BREAKFAST.

The old man and the boy were visiting a second oasis, a very large one, where they had arrived early the previous evening with the other men. This would be their last major stop and final opportunity for rest, refreshment, and re-supply before the remaining two or three days of their journey to Cairo. They were especially glad to replenish their water supply, which had been dwindling more than expected.

Walid was walking alone across a large open area some distance away from their tent. He began to hear loud sounds coming from behind a small building that was on the far perimeter of the oasis, an area surrounded by a dense cluster of palms and bushes. There were muffled shouts, loud grunts, a noise of scuffling, and sharp reports of what could be wood hitting wood. *Crack! Pop! Crack!*

He ran toward the noise and around the side of the building, dodging a cluster of scrub bushes and trees, and suddenly froze in place. He couldn't believe what he was seeing. His heart was pounding hard at the sight that now presented itself so unexpectedly, and his mind nearly stopped.

There was a blur of action. A vicious upper cut was blocked with a thud. One man pushed the other with great strength. The adversary, now off balance, swung a large stick fast toward the head of his attacker. A quick move alone made it miss.

Walid stood there in shock, staring, with his mouth wide open. "Masoon! Hamid! Stop! Stop! Please stop! What are you doing?"

The two men right away lowered their arms and turned toward the boy. Each of them held a long, thick pole made of wood. Their breathing was loud and labored. Masoon bent over for a second with his right hand on his knee, then raised that hand and spoke.

"Oh! Walid, hello! There's no reason to be alarmed. We're fine. We're just exercising our minds and bodies with vigor on this good day."

The boy was practically shaking with the emotion of what he had just thought he was seeing. His stomach still felt like it was trying to leap into his throat. "Oh! I was afraid you were really fighting!"

Both men laughed. Hamid said, "Oh, no, no. Things are not what they seem. I would never take on Masoon in a fight, no matter what he did! I would gather a large army first, and send them to deal with him, while myself watching with trepidation from a great distance, and in possession of a solid alibi."

Masoon chuckled again. "Funny."

Hamid took a moment to catch his breath. "We're just practicing our fighting skills. I learn much from the big man every time we do this."

Masoon still smiled. "And I benefit greatly from Hamid's quick reflexes. He's unusually strong and fast. He gives me a good workout. That's why we exercise together as often as we can."

The boy stepped a bit closer. "I've never seen you do this."

"We've walked off into the desert, on occasion, to practice what we're doing today, normally well away from camp and out of sight, beyond the dunes. And we've gone apart from the others, but closer by, to wrestle several times on this trip. That's fairly quiet, compared to this. I'm sorry we alarmed you."

"Thanks, Masoon. It was my fault. I was just badly misled by appearances. I should have known better. I know both of you well enough to understand that you're very good friends, not enemies. I'm the one who should apologize, for interrupting you."

"No, no, not at all. But you're all right, now?"

"I'm fine. Well, as soon as my heart slows down, I'll be fine." Walid patted his chest. His body was still experiencing the results of the fright, but his mind had calmed down right away, as soon as he understood. He then started to turn away but stopped and said, "Before I go, and let you get back to it, though, could I ask a question?"

"Certainly," Hamid said.

"Ok. Why exactly do you do things like this?"

Masoon replied, "For two reasons, my friend. But, Hamid, you're the doctor. Tell him the medical reason."

The slightly younger man put one end of his long stick on the ground, leaned on it, and explained, "Exercise is the central principle of growth and vitality. We exercise our minds and bodies because, if we don't, they become stagnant, then they began to decay and get weak. But if we use them and strain them and work them well, they become strong and many good things can be ours, including robust health."

Masoon seemed impressed with Hamid's answer. He turned to Walid and said, "It's nice to have a doctor with us. He explains things well, and if he ever gets me good with that stick, he can also fix me up right away."

Both men laughed again.

Walid looked at Hamid and replied, "But wait. I understand that you were exercising your bodies with the sticks, but how were you exercising your minds?"

Hamid responded immediately. "Every skill calls upon the mind. We certainly exercise our minds by reading good books and having deep discussions, but also when we play games requiring complex actions, strategies, and tactics, as well as when we practice our fighting skills, like we were doing, just now. The mind needs this form of exercise as much as the body does. It helps us to stay sharp and quick."

"I'm afraid I still don't fully get it. How exactly is this an exercise of the mind?" The boy was never without questions.

Masoon put his stick to the ground and answered. "What you just saw us doing requires intense concentration and unconscious mental calculations made within a tiny split second. We must be constantly aware of everything around us, to the maximal degree, and decide our next move like lightning.

This trains the mind to work quickly without deliberation, hesitation, or pause. Otherwise, one of us would indeed need a doctor as good as my friend, here."

Walid smiled. He said, "Ok, that makes sense." He was starting to wrap his mind around these things. And he found that this line of thought intrigued him. But another question suddenly arose. And not being one to miss a chance to learn something, he said, "Hamid, I've never asked, but I'm curious about something else as well."

"Sure. Ask."

"Why do you, a trained medical doctor, travel with us to market, rather than staying behind to tend the sick people at home?"

He replied, "Don't worry, my friend. I prepare for these trips. I have a helper in the village who can take over and do most of my work for the sick and injured while I'm gone. And, of course, your father's still there doing his work. He and I have together developed a few special medicines that are unusually effective, and I take these now and then to the city, to give some to the hospital for the poor, and to sell some to other doctors for their wealthier patients, just like you'll be selling things at the market, with Ali. I'm also here in case any of the other men might need my attention along the way."

Masoon spoke up and said, "We're exceptionally blessed by this. It's beneficial in many ways to have a doctor with us. You never know what might happen in the desert. Remember the viper you saw days ago. Hamid can treat any of us who might have a bad encounter with such a creature, or anyone who may undergo some other kind of unforeseen accident or problem. A man can fall from a camel and break an arm or a leg. Health difficulties of other sorts also happen from time to time, and the desert is otherwise quite inhospitable when you have a serious medical need."

The boy nodded. "I'm sure glad you're with us, Hamid, and I know my uncle is, too. He's older, of course, and I think he's extra comforted by your presence." Hamid smiled and nodded silently.

Walid seemed to be thinking deeply for a moment. "Masoon, I believe I understand what you and Hamid have said, that exercise can make the mind and body strong. But you mentioned that there are two reasons you do so much of this exercise. What's the second one?"

Masoon shrugged. "The other reason is to prepare myself for anything challenging or unfortunate that might happen."

"What do you mean?"

"Well, suppose one of our bigger men broke his leg, or was bitten by a viper. I want to be strong enough to carry him to safety, however far that might be, and bring him to Hamid, if that's required. And, if worse trouble were ever to come, I have to be ready for that, as well."

"What kind of trouble?"

"I'm sure you remember a few days ago at breakfast when we discussed the bandits who are in the desert."

"I do remember."

"I've had to take care of that sort of trouble, at least in the past, from time to time."

"Ah, yes, I've heard, Masoon. You're known for that. But, I have another question."

"You do?" Masoon and Hamid looked at each other and both smiled.

The boy had a serious expression. "I do. And it concerns me."

"What is it?"

"I'm still young. How can I take care of any kind of bad trouble if it comes to me and you're not around, and if Hamid's not nearby, either?"

Masoon looked a bit more serious. He said, "Well, you must learn to do and master a few very important things."

"What are they? Can you tell me?"

"Yes. Certainly. Every good working man has a toolkit that contains the tools of his trade. I have a toolkit of wisdom for dealing with trouble."

"You do?"

"Yes. The toolkit is a formula, or a recipe."

"What do you mean?" Walid asked.

The big man replied, "There are six things you need, six tools for dealing with the possibility of trouble, and they break down into three pairs of actions—three doubles, so to speak. And because of that, I call this formula, The Triple Double for Dealing with Trouble. The actions are: Prepare, Perceive; Anticipate, Avoid; Concentrate, and Control. It's that simple."

Walid was eager, as always, to understand. "This toolkit, The Triple Double, and these wisdom tools—can you explain them to me, and how they will be of help for dealing with difficulty, or bad trouble?"

"Surely, my friend, if Hamid doesn't mind."

The doctor smiled again and said, "Let's take a break from

our time of exercise. We can sit and talk. I also want to hear Masoon explain the formula, which is a very good one that I also employ."

Masoon said, "That's an excellent idea. Let's make this an official break." He then put down his pole and sat exactly where he had stood. The doctor sat a few feet away. And Walid came in closer to join them, settling down also on the now already warm sand.

Masoon stretched out his arms and he began to speak. He flashed three fingers, then two at the appropriate moments as he said, "So, I will explain to you The Triple Double for Dealing with Trouble.

"First, prepare. We know that trouble comes to us all in life. That's no surprise. What can be a surprise is when it may visit, and the form it might take. Those things, we often don't know. So we're best served by preparing in advance to meet anything that could come our way, at any time. It's always better to prepare. A sound mind and a strong body, well exercised and expertly skilled, are better able to deal with trouble, or anything else, than a lazy brain and a weak body.

"Nothing ever challenges and develops you unless it stretches you. You must then prepare yourself to be stretched, and this way you'll not likely be torn asunder. Strengthen yourself. Push yourself. Develop physical power and stamina. No one will typically confront you with the prospect of bodily harm unless he thinks he's prepared to dispatch you easily. So you must be even more prepared for him. That way, you'll be providing your own element of surprise as well as the protection that comes from strength."

"I see." Walid looked impressed. Masoon continued.

"This is why Hamid and I develop ourselves with strenuous exercise, and not just basic muscle building and endurance training, but with many advanced warrior skills, which are important for us to have.

"So, first, you prepare your body and mind to be strong and well trained, as you've seen us doing. Start today. Engage in exercises supporting your own body weight. Do pushups. Work the core of your body, around the abdomen. Lift heavy items, various sorts of weights, but do so carefully. Strengthen your legs. We'll show you some things you can do, wherever you are. That way, you can prepare.

"Then, it's also vital for you to take care to perceive well your surroundings at all times. Prepare and perceive—this is the first double. You should perceive like you breathe, but even more. Always be perceptually aware of whatever is near and even far away. Whenever you're awake, you're aware. Even when you sleep, a part of your mind is on guard. And when you're not asleep, you're constantly alert, paying attention at all times to your circumstances and any new developments around you, however small and subtle they might be."

"That sounds like a lot of work," Walid remarked.

Masoon smiled. "It can be at first, but then it becomes second nature, like breathing, an effortless thing you just do. It's simply the way you are in the world. It's a wise way of being."

"I see."

"You watch people. You listen. You sense things. You heed your gut, the instincts and intuitions you have, however slight they may be. You don't sleep walk through life, as most people do. You never forget your need for awareness. You make sure your perceptions are keen and complete. Then, almost nothing will take you by total surprise. You'll perceive some hint, an early indication, or a lead-up, even if it's small, to nearly any threat or trouble that comes your way, if you're always alert and completely conscious. And then you can prepare in a more particular way for any threat you've noticed.

"Prepare. Perceive. That is the first double of the Triple Double. Does this make sense to you?"

The boy answered, "Yes, indeed, it does. It makes complete sense. So, what's next?"

Masoon said, "Then we begin our next pair of actions, our next double—Anticipate and avoid. First: Anticipate. What you see and hear and otherwise sense will give you hints as to what may come next. And you have to use those hints to anticipate what can develop. Not all threats are so obvious that they're seen easily or clearly. Don't be oblivious to the possibilities that lie hidden within any situation. Learn how to quickly extrapolate, infer, and anticipate what could come your way. Then you'll never be completely blind-sided, stunned, and unready to react in an appropriate manner. Those who don't anticipate well don't often survive to do well and flourish."

Walid could not resist interrupting. "You've just used some words I'm not sure about. What does it mean to be oblivious? And then to extrapolate, or infer? I'm not clear on the meanings of these words."

"Oh, yes. Sorry. I easily forget your age. You're so advanced in many ways. But these words are unfamiliar. To be oblivious is to be blind to a situation. You must never turn a blind eye or a deaf ear to what's going on around you. At all times, you need to be keenly attuned to your surroundings. Never be oblivious. And to extrapolate is to project from what you see or otherwise know, to what is, as of yet, unseen, and to what might soon also be. To infer is to draw a conclusion. I infer from your question that you're paying great attention to what I'm saying. And I can extrapolate from this that you'll remember my words."

"I understand now. And, yes, you infer and extrapolate well."

The men looked at other with big smiles. They were always impressed by the boy's quick mind. Masoon said, "Good. My point is that it's important to understand your present in such a way that you can peer into future possibilities and likelihoods, if only for the next few moments. Then you can arrange yourself properly, in your surroundings, to respond."

"But, Uncle Ali has told me that I should learn to live in the present and not dwell too much on the past or the future."

"Your uncle is right. We live in the present with full attention, but with that attention, we can anticipate what may be next without dwelling on it, or obsessing or worrying about it. Anticipation is a form of readiness that's completely compatible with a full attention to, and even an enjoyment of, the present."

"Oh. Ok. I think I now see what you mean."

"Good. And your understanding of all this will grow, as you do it. So, you must learn to anticipate. And you must also learn to avoid. This is the second element in the second double, and completes it."

"Anticipate and avoid." Walid repeated the words.

"Yes," Masoon answered. "And the idea is crucial. Avoid. The key to dealing with most potential troubles in life is to stay far from them. You prepare, perceive, and anticipate, and then you must know how to evade and dodge the possible difficulty that could otherwise be harmful. Avoid it. Be elusive. Stay away. Keep your distance. Most of self-defense is just this: evasive avoidance. It's good to win a battle, if you have to fight. But it's normally better not to fight at all, if it's a potential skirmish you can avoid."

"Ok, I see what you're saying. But how can I do that? How can I get out of the way and escape trouble when it's quickly coming to me?" Walid was intently engaged in what Masoon was saying.

"It's often easier than you might think. If you can anticipate well enough in advance any situations in which trouble may develop, you give yourself the time you need to be able to avoid those difficulties. Eluding trouble is first of all just about staying as far as you can from dangerous situations. And there are general rules. For example, here are some simple ones: Try to avoid walking alone late at night in questionable parts of the city, where we're going to be soon. Trouble often comes late, to hide from the light. And even during the day, if you notice any suspicious characters on one side of the street, then use the other side of the street instead, or take the opportunity to turn aside and visit a shop. Divert your path to a different route, with more people around, where you won't be walking into the trouble that you can see coming your way."

"Oh, Ok, I get it."

"This is a part of wisdom that philosophers call prudence. And there are many such rules. For example: If you witness a person begin to grow angry, say something kind, or excuse yourself courteously, and get out of the situation. Avoid displaying wealth or desirable objects in public when you're alone, or with perhaps only one companion. Don't call unwanted attention to yourself, anything that might make you a target. Avoid the company of troubled people who seem to attract difficulties and disasters. Common sense and a keen awareness can guide you well with such basic principles."

Walid said, "That's a lot to worry about."

"No, no," Masoon answered. "This is not about worry at all. When you learn to be careful in life, when you become a suitably cautious person, overall, it becomes a part of you, a natural way of being in the world, and it actually keeps you from having to worry."

"It does?"

"Yes! You naturally avoid most of the situations that a careless person should indeed worry about!"

Walid looked impressed. "I see. That makes sense. But I still have a concern."

"What is it?"

"If I have lots of rules about what to avoid and where not to go and what not to do, doesn't that mean I'm restricting myself and taking away my own freedom?"

"You take away only your freedom to be likely victimized, and I don't think that's a freedom anyone would actually want." Masoon smiled again and said, "Look. I'm not talking about living in a burdensome and terribly restricted way. I'm just pointing to the importance of simple prudence, or sensible caution—living with awareness, and taking care of yourself in a most obvious way. When you follow some basic rules of trouble avoidance, you can have much more freedom to live happily and in a way that's truly carefree."

Walid replied, "Ok. I get what you're saying." And yet, right then, he suddenly looked skeptical and said to the famous warrior, "But, wait. Masoon, I can't imagine you, of all people, going out of your way to obey these rules and avoid possible trouble."

"Oh, yes, my boy. We have only so much energy in this life. We can't be stumbling into trouble left and right. Even the strongest and bravest men must learn the skill of avoidance. It saves your strength for where it's really needed. And it prevents the harm to others that might come from having to defend yourself unnecessarily. Only foolish people frequently fall into bad trouble. A wise man, however strong, learns to deflect a hostile word with kindness, defuse a tense situation with a smile, and defer to others when that leads him to avoid a fight that's really not needed at all. Most potentially threatening situations can be seen from afar, like a storm in the desert, and can be avoided by prompt and proper action."

"I'd never thought of it like that. And what you say seems wise."

"Good."

"Uncle Ali was recently telling me that most dangers have warnings associated with them that we can perceive, if we're only paying attention."

Hamid spoke up and said, "He's right, as always."

Walid looked over at Masoon, who nodded his agreement, and then he thought for a second more and said, "So, Masoon, if I understand, you've now explained two parts of the Triple Double. I must prepare and perceive, then anticipate and avoid. What comes next in your formula for dealing with trouble?"

The big man cocked his head to one side and raised his bushy eyebrows, lifting his large hands in a bit of a gesture. "Some trouble can't be avoided, however hard we try. It's too determined on its course. It won't give up. It insists on coming up to us. Then we must concentrate our minds and actions in order to handle it well. We can't be torn by worries, anxieties, doubts, or fears. We need to focus our entire minds and bodies on the challenge we face, whatever it is, seeing how it can be met and conquered, and then doing what we know must be done."

"This also rings true," Walid replied.

"So, the first key of double number three is: Concentrate."

"But, really, how can I concentrate my mind if I'm afraid or worried?"

"I believe your uncle has told you much about the power of the mind."

"Yes, he has."

"Well, this is one way that the mind's power benefits us greatly. It's normal, when in danger, to feel fear. A great man trains himself to be aware of the fear as just one more fact for his consideration, and one that can be dismissed, or changed and overcome, when appropriate, with a proper concentration of the mind. When we deliberately take action and concentrate properly, in any such situation, directing our thoughts in a productive way, we can calm our emotions and marshal our powers and skills to the greatest extent. Appropriate action of any sort helps concentrate the mind.

"Most adversaries will not have the habit of disciplined concentration in their arsenal. Those of us who do, most often prevail. Violent or treacherous people typically act on waves of emotion. They're not stable or well focused. Most difficult situations of any sort can be handled by a strongly focused concentration of thought and action that directs your energy to pour forth at exactly the right time and into just the right place to allow you to prevail. This is what Hamid and I practice together, in, for example, what you just saw us doing."

"This factor of concentration seems very important."

"It is."

"But there's also one more thing, beyond concentration?"

"Yes, here is where we complete The Triple Double. There's the matter of: Control. We must first control ourselves—or get a grip on any emotions and reactions not already tamed by our concentration. We can't allow any fear or excitement or anger to get the best of us."

"How can I do this?"

"Take a deep breath, relax your muscles for even a moment, and empty your thoughts of anything extraneous. You can become very skilled at doing this. And these actions can then create a measure of inner calm in the midst of even dire trouble. Always remember the importance of your mind for overcoming challenges, and the crucial nature of self-control for using well the power that you have. This allows you to act effectively and decisively. Control your emotions, control your thoughts, and then you're better positioned to control the situation around you."

Walid said, "I was talking to Uncle Ali the other day about self control. He seems to have so much more than I do. I'd like to get better at it."

Hamid spoke up again and said, "Well, self control is sometimes called will-power. And it's a little like the power of a muscle. You can build it up, and you can deplete it. The more you need to use it in a given day, the more difficult it gets. It's almost as if you can weaken your power of will the way you can exhaust the strength of a muscle, by repeated use, or overuse. Too many people diminish their self control by making every little thing a big deal, every decision a monumental event, and in doing that, they reduce their ability to exercise control when it's really needed. If you learn how to relax during the ordinary course of things, then when the extraordinary challenge does occur, you'll be more likely to have the degree and strength of self control available that you need."

"That's a new way of thinking about self control," Walid remarked.

Hamid commented, "And it seems quite effective. But I should let Masoon finish his explanation, which he's giving us with great clarity."

Masoon smiled again and nodded. "Ok, then. We're discussing, at this point, control. When trouble has arrived, we first need to control ourselves. Then, we need to control the situation that confronts us, as much as we can. Don't let it get out of hand. Take charge. Contain it. Keep it as manageable as possible. Don't permit a small fire to grow into a broader conflagration. Solve a problem when it's just appearing, and is still so small that you can hardly notice it. Don't wait until it's big and out of control. The ancients have taught us about this. When a problem is hard to spot, it's often easy to solve; but when it's easy to spot, it's often hard to solve.

"Keep your difficulties contained and under control. If one angry man confronts you, deal with him in a way that doesn't make him call five of his friends into the situation. You might be able to diffuse his anger, or distract his attention. Or, if that doesn't work, and he becomes physical, you may have to deal with his wrath in a physical way yourself. But whatever you do, seek to control the situation. Don't allow it to escalate into something you can't guide or govern."

Walid spoke up. "But aren't there many things we can't control?"

"Yes. And that's inevitable. We can't control life in general, or all aspects of the day we're now living, but we can often do something to form or mold whatever the day brings to us, by governing how we react to it and what we do about it. There's normally a way to exercise some degree of positive management in even the most negative situation. When you can find that, and then do it, you can accomplish great things, even amid raging storms of trouble."

"I understand," Walid replied. "You've explained this very well."

"Good."

"It seems deep and important."

"It is. And I'm glad you see that. I know you and Ali have spoken of what he rightly calls "the oasis within" that we can carry with us everywhere we go—that deep place of calm protection and inner resources that we can cultivate for our lives."

"Yes. Uncle has told me a lot about this oasis. And I'm beginning to feel that I have it within me."

"Good. That's very good. And what we have now spoken of is also a part of that."

"It is?"

"Yes. Having always the Triple Double among your habits of thought and action, and thus your resources, helps to create and preserve that oasis."

"Wow. That makes sense."

"So, I should sum up what I've said: This is my toolkit for trouble, my little formula. The Triple Double will help in trouble, even if you face ... double trouble!" Masoon then laughed heartily. Walid and Hamid both grinned at his cleverness.

Hamid said, "I like this idea of a wisdom toolkit, Masoon. I've not heard it put in this way before. It's a useful image. I believe in The Triple Double, and admire your explanation of it to our young friend. Prepare, perceive; anticipate, avoid; concentrate, control. It's an important set of actions to understand, and to train yourself in doing—very important, indeed."

"Thank you, kind doctor. Your words are medicine for the soul."

Walid then said, "Masoon, did you make up all of this yourself?"

He laughed and said, "Oh, no, not at all. These ideas have been handed down through generations of wise men I admire. I merely seek to live their legacy to the fullest. You see, many great people have traveled this world before us and have left us their insights for living well. We benefit by using their best ideas about life. We don't have to make it all up ourselves. Wisdom such as this is a bit like the contents of a big treasure chest that's our proper inheritance. There's great advice available to us because it's been handed down to us, and it involves insight about many things. This particular wisdom about trouble has served me well throughout my life. The ideas are old. It's only my formulation and statement of them that's a little new."

The boy sat in thought as the men looked at him to see what his next reaction might be.

He suddenly seemed puzzled by something. And, as always, he didn't hesitate to express what was bothering him. "But, why are there so many troubles throughout life in the first place?"

Hamid spoke instantly. "We sometimes forget that you're so much of a philosopher, my friend. You like to go deep. And we do, too. So I can tell you this: First, you should consider the immense complexity of nature, as a whole. It's astonishingly powerful in many ways. Its forces bring us much delight, and much danger, and trouble, as well. In addition, there is human nature, a small part of the overall picture. And it has great power. We human beings have minds and free will. This is, of course, a great good, and it allows for terrible ill."

The boy saw instantly how this answered his question. He

said, "Yes. Uncle Ali has also talked to me about the two powers in our world."

"I remember. And it's a vital lesson. There are many things with power to help and equal power to harm, power for good and, likewise, power for ill. That allows for many great joys in this world and many difficulties and sorrows, too." Hamid looked over at Masoon, who then spoke as well.

"This is a very interesting issue, and even profound, I think. I've never known a happy man without much trouble in his life. And I've never known an unhappy man without much good in his life. Walid, what does your uncle say about the things that come into our lives, the things that happen to us?"

The boy replied eagerly. "It doesn't matter so much what happens to us as how we think about what happens to us. And he says that we can't control the day but only what we make of the day."

Masoon nodded. "That's correct. And it's wise. For those of us in the fellowship of the mind, it's the crucial thing. Our troubles, those that insist on visiting us, if we react to them well, create more growth in us as people. Our greatest difficulties exercise us the most. They make us stronger and deeper and more complete and better. A man with no real trouble at all would be no real man at all. And great women are exactly the same."

Hamid then added, "Life must sometimes be hard, or it's hardly a life."

Masoon nodded vigorously, and the doctor continued. "Hard times prepare us for happy times. The worst of times can make possible the best of times. Tough situations can create in us terrific virtues without which we could not flourish and ultimately be happy in the world. Great pain can indeed bring great gain, as people often remark."

Walid smiled. "You two have many clever sayings, like my uncle."

Hamid shook his head in agreement. "We probably stole them from your uncle."

Masoon said, "Don't let that get back to him or trouble indeed would be on the way."

They all shared a good laugh and a gratifying inner sense of thoughts well developed, and lessons well shared.

There is a deep satisfaction in talking of important things with a serious intent, but also a light heart, and in a good fellowship of understanding. Wisdom is a friend of the spirit and welcomes us all into its circle whenever we desire its help and companionship on our journeys. It gives us a foundation for our own oasis within, a refreshing place of rest and restoration that we can indeed take with us wherever we go.

The boy now sat there on the sand with a sense of fascination and even delight. He felt more prepared than ever for any difficulties that might come his way. And that gave him a new measure of inner confidence. He thought for a second that it's too bad this portion of the trip is almost over. He had been learning so much. And he had already been using many of the new insights that were coming his way. He could have no way of knowing how many more he'd be called on to use very soon.

He would have to go back to the tent right away and find his uncle and tell him about this great conversation and all that he'd picked up from these two good friends. He then smiled as he thought, "Uncle Ali will love this."

And he was right. Ali would be glad, and then later greatly relieved that Walid had been so well prepared for the bad trouble that was about to appear, and that would be the most serious of their lives.

12

AN UNEXPECTED REVELATION

SOMETIMES TROUBLE IS SLOW TO DEVELOP, BUT QUICK TO STRIKE.

The old man was having the deepest sleep of his life. Many voices could be heard in the distance. The boy was also still fully asleep. Suddenly, the tent flap was pulled back by a man named Jazeer.

"Ali! Ali!"

It was as if he had been raised up from a deep abyss. "Yes?"

"Faisul is gone! And three camels are missing!"

"What about the things the camels were carrying?'

"He left some of the bags behind, but took one that had been on Masoon's camel, the special bag!"

"I see. Go get Masoon and Hamid immediately. We must take action. And tell Bancom to ride like the wind. He'll know what to do."

Jazeer said, "Masoon and Hamid left the oasis a bit earlier for their exercise, before the discovery was made. I'll find them. But I'll speak to Bancom right now."

The boy had been awakened from a profound sleep by the first urgent words of the announcement. He listened to everything and then said, "Uncle, what's going on?"

"Don't worry." Ali began putting on his sandals.

The boy rubbed his eyes. "Why would that man Faisul leave secretly with three camels? Is he a camel thief?"

"No, my boy, it's likely much more serious than that."

"What do you mean?"

The old man took a deep breath and said in a low voice, "There's a strong chance that Faisul is a traitor."

"I don't understand."

"There's something I should tell you. I had planned to do so when the time was right, sometime soon, in the next few months, and with your parents, when we were back home. But, in light of this development, the time must now be right." Ali gently put his hand on top of the boy's foot, and patted it, in a gesture of loving reassurance.

"What is it? This sounds serious."

"It is, but it's not bad. It's good. Do you remember the night we talked about your being a prince or a king in the realm of your mind?"

"Yes, I remember everything you said."

"I mentioned that there were things yet to be revealed."

"Yes, you did."

"One of those things is about me and your father. And it's about you."

"What do you mean?"

The old man looked into the boy's eyes. And he spoke with a calm, soft voice. "My father was king. And his father was king. Back through time, my ancestors were kings. Your father, of course, is my brother. So his father, your grandfather, was once king of the realm."

"The realm of the mind that you were telling me about?"

"Well, yes, and also in the world more broadly, in our realm of earthly politics, over our kingdom."

"You mean, of Egypt?"

"Yes."

"My grandfather was The King of Egypt?

"Yes."

"How can this be?"

Ali took a deep breath and said, "There were some terrible things that happened when I was a boy. My mother told me all about them when I was older. My father was killed in a palace uprising. The man who had served as treasurer to the kingdom plotted to gain control and make himself king. He gave promises to others to win their support. Your grandfather was much loved, but a group of men overcome with greed committed heinous deeds to forcibly take his throne. A few loyal insiders helped my mother, the queen, to escape at night with me and a few of her retainers and friends. At the time, she didn't yet know that she was carrying within her another child, who was later to be born and eventually become your father."

Walid sat in rapt silence, stunned, and trying to take it all in.

"But no one's ever told me any of this."

"For your protection, and to allow you to have a normal childhood, we had to wait as long as we could. Faisul may have set in motion some events now that require you to know what's going on." The old man began to gather up things in the tent as he continued to speak, with his kind gaze still mainly on Walid.

"Your father was born in exile. Your grandmother vowed that she would prepare us to take our proper places one day in the life of the kingdom. I would be king and your father would be the prince, my closest ally and, in a sense, co-regent for all the affairs of the kingdom. There has always been strong support for our return, ever since those unfortunate events happened and became known."

"I don't know what to say."

"I'm sure that all of this comes as a great surprise. And I'm sorry it's so sudden. When I was a little older than you are now, all of it was explained to me. And then later, when your father also came to the proper age, our mother told him of his heritage, as she had told me. He seemed certain from the first, though, that helping rule the kingdom would not in fact be his destiny, but rather would fall entirely to me. But then, one day, it would become the mission of a son he would eventually be blessed to have. This son would return to the role that his forebears had always served. And you are the son."

Walid felt the strangest he had ever felt in his entire life. It was almost as if time had slowed down while he was hearing all this. He said, "Uncle Ali, coming from anyone other than my parents or you, this would be completely impossible to believe. But I trust what you say, even though it's so incredible and such a shock that I can barely think through what it means. Why didn't my father want to help you rule?"

"Your father has always been very strong in body and mind. He was quietly given an exceptional education to prepare him for whatever the future might require. And, in the course of his learning, he felt a sense of calling, and decided that he wanted to serve those around him as a medical doctor. He became a physician to the average man, and to the poor. He grew to be the generous benefactor that you've always known him to be."

"He does have a strong sense of mission."

"Yes. You've seen how he works with Hamid in the village, and in all the surrounding territory. And he's not just a doctor of the body. He's always helped in every aspect of his patients' lives. He saw this role as a true calling and a life mission that he was not to abandon for any reason. But he also understood the destiny that would flow through him and his choices. Before he married your mother, he confided to her all these things, so that she would know the full picture of his life, and what a commitment to him might involve. She agreed to support him in every way and to help educate any children they might have, in such a manner that the kingdom could be restored and maintained."

"What does the man Faisul have to do with all this?"

"In a bag that Faisul has taken, there's money and what appear to be many valuable jewels of great price. But they're not real gems. These things are in the bag to allow a traitor to think that if he steals the bag, we'll believe him to be merely a thief. Then, he also took two extra camels, most likely to reinforce what he thinks to be his deception."

"I don't understand."

Ali continued, "A few days ago at breakfast, it was Faisul who brought up the topic of bandits and thieves in the desert, perhaps to plant the idea of such things in our minds, so that when he left with camels and Masoon's bag, simple theft would be the first thing we'd think. But the real reason he's taken the bag, and the most important thing in the bag, is a letter in an unsealed envelope that's addressed to Masoon, and marked for his eyes only."

"What's in the envelope?"

"A letter that instructs Masoon to take a second and larger envelope, also within the bag, along with the money and jewels, to friends of the rightful king who are currently serving in high administrative positions in the palace. The large envelope is addressed by name to those two men. In it is a message that this is the week when a long planned internal uprising should occur. And it goes on to direct them as to what they should do to secure the palace for our return."

"Faisul has this in his possession? With the names? That's terrible!"

The old man's face was placidly calm. "Remember the morning of the storm, my boy, when everything looked so nice?"

"Yes. But, wait. Do you mean that this is not what it seems, either?"

The old man nodded. "Yesterday, you told me that Masoon had explained to you The Triple Double."

"Yes. Prepare, Perceive; Anticipate, Avoid; Concentrate,

Control."

"You remember well, as always. It's our habit to do all these things. There are two purposes for our camel train, our little caravan of merchants and traders crossing the desert. One, as you know, is to bring our goods to market. The other is to meet with our friends and confederates in the palace and around the city to prepare for a coming restoration of the proper monarchy. We've been doing our diligent planning under the cover of normal commerce for a few years now. And we've always known that we had to prepare for trouble, to be perceptive as things might unfold, to anticipate what could happen to foil our plans, and act so as to avoid the worst results of such threats, if possible. We have concentrated on what it would take to keep our plans alive, and have sought to create what might be needed to control any act of interference."

The boy started to ask a question, but Ali held up two fingers and continued. "You remember the principle of the two powers."

"Things that have power to help often also have power to harm."

"This is our fifth caravan as a group to the capital city. It's been very useful for us to make these trips, and yet at the same time quite dangerous. Without reasonable risk, there can be no great reward. We've always known it to be possible that one of our companions might, out of personal weakness, greed, or inappropriate ambition, choose to betray our cause. It seems now that this falls to Faisul, the newest member of our group. He's been helpful to us in various ways since he joined us, but he appears now intent on being harmful."

"Did you suspect that Faisul might be a traitor?"

"Since he came to us, we've noticed that he's a nervous man, not normally comfortable around the rest of us. He's always been a bit of a different sort, who certainly says many of the right things, but he often behaves strangely. When words and deeds don't align, it's usually a troubling sign. So, this is not entirely unexpected. There were many small warnings, however slight."

"That's just like what you said about the viper, Uncle. You taught me that when he approaches, he makes warning sounds of which he may be unaware."

"Yes, indeed. Many of us recognized that Faisul was a bit odd, and something of an outsider who seemed to be going out of his way to look like he fit in. We prepared ahead of time a bit of a ruse, a little trick, in case there was anyone, and especially him, planning to betray us."

Walid said, "I'm guessing the ruse involves the bag that he took, in a way that goes beyond just containing false jewels."

"That is correct, my friend. We made it clear to all the men that this particular bag was for Masoon only, and its contents for his eyes only. A traitor, knowing that Masoon is our top warrior, would easily suspect that there were plans for war, or incriminating documents of some sort about our intended revolution, inside the bag."

"I see."

"And, you now know that Masoon often disappears, for a time, on many days, sometimes near camp, and occasionally a distance away, to do his exercises with Hamid. He tells everyone they need solitude and silence for this purpose. But he also goes off to allow any traitor among us to have an opportunity to examine the bag."

"Oh, that's clever."

"One day, Masoon actually asked Faisul to watch the bag for him, saying he planned extensive workouts and would be gone a long while. He even suggested that Faisul take the bag into his own tent for safekeeping, perhaps allowing him to form the impression that he was specially trusted."

"Then Faisul opened the bag?"

"Apparently, he did, and read enough to think he knows what it contains. He's now on his way, almost certainly, to turn it over to the current king's men and reap a big reward. Even the money and the seemingly valuable jewels in the bag are not likely enough gain for such a one as he."

"But you said that the bag's contents reveal the names of our friends!"

"It has the names of people called friends, but they're actually men who are in fact no friends of ours at all, but rather, enemies—two individuals long suspected by the present king of disloyal intent, men more greedy and ambitious than our poor Faisul. The letter addresses them as if they were our friends and co-conspirators."

"But why did you put their names on the documents and write to them as if they were our friends?"

"When they're wrongly identified as our accomplices inside the palace, they'll be taken out of the way and dealt with harshly. Their fathers were part of the original, unlawful coup that killed your grandfather. And, to an even greater extent than those traitors long ago, these men have never been content with their elevated, but less than supreme, standing in the court. They've always lusted for more, and have recently begun to scheme insurrection for the sake of their own ascension, just like their fathers did."

"That's terrible."

Ali said, "Faisul, in seeking to betray us and our true friends, will actually be helping us. He will make sure that those men, who would otherwise stand in our way, along with any of their known supporters, are removed from the scene. You see again how things can be very different from what they at first seem."

"This is all amazing, Uncle. But won't the king's army still come to attack us when they hear and read about our intentions?"

"The letter in the bag, to our false confederates, states that, in accordance with longstanding plans, they could expect to find us, if they need us early, at a particular spot due west of the city, a day's travel away from it. Here in the oasis, we're a two or three day journey away."

"So we won't be there after all? And they'll go to the wrong place?"

"Yes. It was our prior intent to go through that location, but our plan has now suddenly changed."

"But when they see that we're not there, won't they come here? Won't Faisul have told them that he left us here at the oasis?"

"Indeed, they will come here, but when they arrive, we'll no longer be present. Later on this morning, as soon as we can, we'll leave to the south, get away from the oasis, and then alter course, to the west and then to the north. We'll finally turn east, and we'll pass this place at a distance. At that point we can approach the city by a route where there are some rocky hills and outcroppings that allow for good defenses, in case anyone with hostile intent should come across us."

The boy nodded, taking it all in. He said, "So, when any soldiers get here to the oasis, they'll be told that we've already left, and are going to the south?"

"Yes."

"But won't they be able to follow our tracks and eventually see that we turned several times?"

"The wind that carries so much information also happily erases many things as well, especially signs that exist only in the desert sand."

"Oh."

The old man continued. "Bancom will be riding by a different route into the city, one that's much shorter. And even though it's harder to travel, he'll be on a swift horse that we've brought for this purpose. Our camel thief has three slow beasts to govern his pace. He'll be limited by the slowest of them. By the time he gets into the city to provide his information, and the king's soldiers, as a result, have any hope of trying to locate us in the vastness of the desert, we'll likely have arrived already in the city ourselves, and with new allies there, we'll have become a much larger force than the party they'll send out in pursuit of our current camel train. We'll likely have entered, and perhaps even taken, the palace itself, with the aid of many friends there, while the soldiers in pursuit of us are out on the sand, and not where they would truly be needed to defend their false king."

"That's an incredible plan!"

"Faisul was easy. If you make a good enough trap, an eager bird will snare itself. The rest of it took some creative thought."

"How did you know all this would happen?"

"We never knew, in fact, but we had to be ready for anything. It was at least possible that such a betrayal would happen. As I mentioned, we've always followed The Triple Double. We prepare well, perceive closely, anticipate all likelihoods, seek to avoid the trouble that we can, concentrate on what needs to be done, and work to control whatever we're able to control."

"Wow. I see how it all works, now, in a real situation."

"We use what we have—our wits, a horse, a package, two documents, our friends, some hard-earned knowledge, and a cool and calming peace that comes from the oasis within our hearts. Then we act with courage, knowing that what we do is right."

"I'm still trying to take in all this that you're telling me, and get my bearings."

"I know it's a lot to hear at once. But it's all important. As we continue to speak of these things, let's leave our tent and walk to where the birds are being kept."

Walid got up from where he had been sitting, and they both slipped out of the tent flap and began to walk to a nearby spot where messenger birds were waiting in a cage covered against the night chill. They could hear a few slight noises as they approached.

Ali uncovered the metal cage, opened its door, and attached something to the legs of three birds. He then waved his hand for them to fly. As they did, he turned to Walid and said, "These creatures of the air are also our friends, and will carry the news to the right places, like Bancom does. Two will fly to the city. One will return to our village, if he can fly unimpeded. They'll all help in different ways to announce and prepare the way for our arrival."

As the old man and the boy stood watching the birds rapidly flap their wings and fly off into the sky, a pair to the east and one messenger to the west, Ali grew pensive and spoke in a very serious and measured tone. "My good friend, I must also share with you something else now, something of a deep philosophical nature. And you need to remember it well."

"I promise I will."

"This is what you must not forget: There is a war in this world between goodness and corruption, between genuine love and untethered lust. Corruption, greed, and blind desire can win a battle now and then, and can even seem to crush their adversaries. But eventually, the good and the true, and the wisely guided, will prevail. Love is the greatest power of all. Only it can endure."

"How can we be sure of this philosophy, Uncle? How can we know this view to be true?"

"Experience is a fine teacher, my boy, but only if you're a careful student will you learn well from it. When you study life in this world, you see many misdeeds appearing to flourish, but this is on the surface of things only. Deep down, the foundations of the world will ultimately support only the good and loving heart. When all is said and done, pure intentions alone will win over all."

"I feel the truth of what you're saying, Uncle. I hope it, but I also believe it. And this is very good."

"That's because your heart is right, my boy, and so is your mind. And it's important that you know this: You'll have many adventures in this life, adventures of gladness and pain, times of victory and defeat, and every experience will make its mark on you, guiding your path forward in ways you can't even imagine right now. But with faith in your heart, and a trust in the process of it all, you'll become what you're meant to be, and accomplish what you're here to do. You have a mission in this world. We all do. And it's up to us to have faith and trust, to cultivate a pure heart, and a strong mind, and to make our best choices each day."

"But what if we make mistakes in our choices, and even big ones?"

"That, too, becomes a part of the process. We learn, we correct, and then we can prosper. Mistakes and failures are not to be feared or felt with embarrassment and shame, but with an open-ness to correction, as a necessary part of the great education the world can provide."

"I can still hardly believe that I'm a real prince and that you, my uncle that I've known all my life, are the rightful king of our land. What I wished to be, I am. But all of my life, until now, I had no idea."

"I know. I understand. And this reflects a general truth. Most people have no idea who they really are. But if they can discover their true nobility, and embrace it with an equally proper humility of spirit, then they can move into a new sense of their privileges and opportunities and responsibilities in the world. Greatness, in some form, awaits."

Just then, Jazeer returned with Masoon and Hamid. The boy could see them approaching together through a grove of nearby palms.

The old man turned to look at them. As they drew closer, all three men surprisingly broke into big smiles. They then stopped together about ten feet away. Masoon spoke directly to Ali.

"Your Majesty: Your throne awaits you." All three men bowed deeply. Then, looking at Walid, he continued to speak.

"Young Prince, your time has come sooner than we had expected." Glancing back over again at Ali and reaching down to his belt, he said, "If I may?"

The old man nodded. Masoon pulled from the many folds of his belt a beautiful small revolver that had been concealed there.

"Prince Walid, I know your father has taught you well, from an early age, in the art of marksmanship and firearm safety. Please accept this as a gift to be tucked into your own belt and carried for extra security." He handed the boy the gleaming gun resting across both his hands, briefly bowed his head in acknowledgment again, and then, took a step back.

As Walid took it into his hands, he said, "This is really for me?"

Masoon replied, "Yes. But you'll not likely need it any time soon. Brains more than bullets, spirits more than swords, will make way the path of the future. May your mind and heart long lead your way properly forward into the brilliant future that's now yours to claim."

Ali had been watching all this. He spoke to the prince.

"It's our job soon to take our proper roles, and work hard to eventually put ourselves out of business, preparing our people for their own royal governance of the land, and themselves, on every level, from the individual, to the tribe and the town, up to the nation. It will be enough for us, and our great honor in the long run, to embody, symbolize, and remind each man and woman of their own exalted place in this world."

Prince Walid Fancoom Shabeezar took a deep breath, and simply looked for a moment at Jazeer, Masoon, Hamid, and finally again at his uncle. Then he spoke to them all as he responded to his uncle. "I'm ready to do my part. I'm prepared for whatever comes my way."

The rightful king replied, "Good man. Good man."

13

SEVEN SECRETS

THE MOST UNEXPECTED ADVENTURE CAN START AT ALMOST ANY TIME.

Transformative events don't often clearly announce themselves in advance. They happen, and we respond. And yet, sometimes, small things begin to come to our attention that will prepare us in subtle ways, beyond our explicit knowing, for something big that awaits only our own readiness. That's exactly what had been happening as Ali and Walid crossed the desert together, up to this point.

The first of many sudden and transformative events on the horizon had now entered their lives. Much had changed in a moment. The journey already underway immediately took on a new purpose. A flexibility of mind and a resilience of attitude allowed everyone to adjust and make the most of the new situation. But concern was still in the air. No one knew with certainty what they would soon face.

The old man and the boy had left the oasis and traveled several hours at this point with their many friends. They moved first to the south, just out of sight, and then doubled back, west and northwest. Their trail then took them due north, then northeast, and east, finally to pass the day's origination point a short distance above it on a map, if there had been a map, and with their faces now at last turned toward the center of power where their destiny was soon to be found. This path for the first hours of travel away from the oasis had traced the figure of something like a half moon, from the top peak and first down the straight side. This was intended to throw off any observers who could be asked to report on the direction of their travel. It would help them evade whatever enemies might seek to find them, while still getting them as quickly as possible, under the circumstances, to where their presence would soon be needed.

The mid-day sun, as always, demanded a rest, even for men in a hurry. Any path of achievement involves both times of action and periods of pause. Often, it's while we wait, with a measure of patience, that we learn what we'll eventually need to know in order to act properly and well. Quickly pitched tents, some cool water, and a small bit of food distributed among the men prepared them all for a short time of repose in the shade they had created.

Walid now lay on his back in the small tent, hands crossed on his chest, fingers loosely interlocked, as he pondered the events of the morning and what was yet to come. It was still hard to get his head around all that was happening. He was overwhelmed, and more than a little apprehensive.

"Uncle, are you worried at all about Faisul and whether your plan for dealing with him will work?"

From his own resting position in their tent, the rightful king spoke softly in reply. "No, I'm not worried. Worry accomplishes nothing. I've considered all the likelihoods, and I'm prepared for whatever may occur. Thinking through the possibilities, the ways in which things can go wrong, along with the alternative ways in which they can go right, empowers us, as long as we don't obsess endlessly about it all."

"I see." Walid really didn't yet see, but he was at least a little assured by his uncle's words.

Ali added, "Your spirit can precede you in new adventures, preparing the way for your body and soul. Wherever you go first in your mind, you can often go best and more safely in your body. Properly projecting forward in our imaginations, in a disciplined way, can smooth the path ahead. But the emotions of worry are different. Anxiety is terribly corrosive. It erodes the soul. It's a poison. It doesn't help us in any way to face the future."

"You say that we can project our imaginations well and productively into the future, while yet still living fully in the present?"

"Yes, my friend. We can rationally anticipate the future while fully dwelling in the present, deep in our hearts. But worry is different. The present bears seeds of the future that we can tend creatively, when we spot them well. But worry pulls us out of the present to a badly imagined scenario that's almost always wrong."

Walid was silent for a moment. "So, you think the plan will work?"

"I do."

"What will happen then, when we arrive in the city?"

"We'll follow the plan, and meet our destiny."

"But what exactly does that mean, Uncle? What is destiny? I've heard it spoken of many times. But I don't really understand it. Is it like fate?"

The old man smiled. "I asked that same question to my mother when I was about your age, or a little younger. She told me that destiny is the combined fruit of what happens to us and what happens because of us. She also helped me understand that what we choose to do is the most important thing for guiding what happens with us."

"How, then, can we guide well the things that involve us?"

"That's a big question, my boy. Do you need to nap now?"

"No, I'm actually wide awake. I need to rest a little, like we're doing now, but not to sleep."

"I feel the same way. So perhaps I can take the time to answer your question with the care it deserves."

"Good, I'm eager for some new understanding, Uncle."

"Have you ever heard of a certain ancient philosophy of seven universal conditions for success in living our adventures well?"

"I don't think I have."

"Wise people throughout history and across cultures have identified seven things, seven facilitating conditions, that raise our likelihood for success in any challenge we face. These seven ideas provide something like a map to guide us forward in how best to use our abilities and energies. Some think of them as a collection of seven secrets for outstanding accomplishment in the world."

"I'm certain now that I've never heard of these things. They're still secrets to me."

"Well, your parents would have explained them to you soon enough, I'm sure. Actually, I would guess, it would have been shortly after this trip. They didn't anticipate that you'd have the opportunity on this journey to help accomplish great things. And so, they had no idea you might need these concepts as part of your equipment for this particular adventure."

"Can you tell me what these ideas are?"

"Yes, certainly." Ali turned over and looked across the small tent at his nephew who was in some ways, even at the age of thirteen, still so young, and yet now stood on the threshold of great events. The old man paused, and seemed to be in contemplation for just a moment, gathering his thoughts and choosing his words carefully. Their tent flaps fluttered in a brisk but still gentle breeze. He then spoke, as the good teacher he was. "In confronting any difficult challenge, or facing any wonderful opportunity, there are seven things we need to bring with us."

"Ok. What do we need?"

Ali laughed and said, "You're my most eager student, ever."

"Good!" Walid couldn't contain his keen interest in learning such things. A spirit of curiosity now animated his features, as it often did.

Ali spoke slowly, and used the fingers of one hand, and then the other, to count off each of the things he was enumerating. He said, "For true success, we need:

(1) a clear conception of what we want, a goal vividly imagined,

(2) a strong confidence that we can attain the goal,

(3) a focused concentration on what it will take to reach this achievement,

(4) a stubborn consistency in pursuing our vision,

(5) an emotional commitment to the importance of what we're doing,

(6) a good character to guide us and keep us on a proper course, and, finally,

(7) a capacity to enjoy the process, along the way."

"Wow. That's a lot to hear at one time. But it sounds important. I need to get out my notebook to put this in my idea diary. It's too much to remember all at once." Walid reached over to a bag lying on the sand near him, and pulled out some of his things for writing. Then he said, "Could you repeat these things for me?"

"Certainly. We need a clear conception of a goal, a strong confidence in our efforts, a focused concentration, a stubborn consistency, an emotional commitment, a good character, and a capacity to enjoy the process of what we're doing, along the way."

"I think I have them now. The seven secrets are: conception, confidence, concentration, consistency, commitment, character, and capacity."

"A capacity to Enjoy," the old man said, making sure that Walid didn't miss the full specificity of what was being stated.

"Although, you're also right that a general capacity is needed for the sort of goal we set, a capacity to pursue and attain it. This is actually a vital but often hidden part of the capacity to enjoy, since you can't fully enjoy the pursuit of something that's simply not right for who you are."

"Oh. That's really interesting."

"Yes, it is. And you're correct, my boy, to see all of this as very important. I've lived my life with the use of these seven conditions." He paused and asked, "Would you like me to say a bit more about each of them?"

"Please do," Walid replied.

Ali said, "Good. So we can begin with an inner mental conception, an appropriate start. We first conceive goals in our minds, and then set them in our hearts."

"And what exactly is a goal? I already know that it's an objective, or anything you're aiming to achieve—something you're desiring and hoping to make happen."

"Good. But there's more. A goal is a decision and a commitment of the will to attain something specific. It's not just a vague idea or a fantasy or a thing of mere hope. It must be something envisioned toward which we work to align our actions and energies. We talk about setting goals, but we are actually setting ourselves on a new path of concentrated, consistent, and committed action. And then, when we attain our goals, we need to set new ones. Our bodies and minds are built to pursue aims that are noble and right for us. Without good targets to shoot at, a person's life is literally aimless."

"I see." Walid was listening with total focus.

At that point, Ali sat up, legs crossed, and facing his

nephew in the shade of their tent. He scratched his chin and thought for a moment.

"This leads me to something else that's important about these ideas, as you consider possible goals for the future."

"Good. I'm keen to learn more about it."

"This is something most people seem not to realize. And it's crucial. When you're considering launching out in a new direction, or pursuing a potential new goal that may be challenging, you first need to use these seven conditions as tests or standards for proceeding. They're something like a checklist. You should ask yourself the question: Can I arrive at a truly clear conception of what I'll be pursuing with such a goal? Will I be able to work toward this with confidence? Is it really something I can focus my concentration on, well, and over time? Can I act consistently with this sort of aim, given the other things I must do? Am I emotionally committed to it? Is it likely that I can press toward it with good character? Do I have, or can I cultivate, a capacity to enjoy the process that pursuing this goal will require?

"If you're uncertain about any of these things, and can't figure out how to get a clear positive answer for all such questions, you should rethink the possible goal and set yourself another one, instead. Then, when you have a proper new goal, one that's right for you, it's time to use all seven conditions to support your endeavor. So these seven ideas are at first a test, and then a tool, for effective goal pursuit."

Walid said, "Interesting. First a test and then a tool."

"Yes. Now, even as a tool, these secrets are meant to test you, to help you examine your mind, heart, and actions. If you can pass the test, you're more likely to succeed, however difficult the challenge may be." The boy listened quietly as the old man went on. "I've used these ideas to help me get things done since I was not much older than you are now. Everything I've accomplished as an adult, I've owed to these secrets. And every time I feel that something's not quite right in my life, I can use this framework of ideas as a diagnostic device—again, as a test of my own actions. There will always be one or two of the conditions that I've perhaps forgotten about, or at least partially ignored, and need to focus on once more."

"Uncle, this explains to me how you can approach any challenge with such a positive attitude. You have all these things working for you."

"You're right. It's because I pay attention to these things that I can be so optimistic in my pursuits."

"Will acting with the ongoing test and tool provided by these seven guides always lead to success and great achievement?"

"Ah! You may be surprised to hear me say: No. I'm afraid not."

Walid laughed and said, "I am surprised!"

The old man explained, "The world just doesn't work like that. There are no simple guarantees for success. Life is complex and full of surprises and no simple formula will ever give you a magical ability to override contrary forces and impose your will on the future with certainty, come what may."

"But then, what do these seven secrets do?"

"No tool can guarantee you what you want. But the right tools can help greatly. These seven conditions will put you into the best possible position for the sort of accomplishment we all desire. They are the most universal and fundamental facilitators of excellence. As such, they can be depended on to give you the best chance, in any circumstances, for some form of success, as you define it, or as may be right for you. They can't promise you success in a particular result, but they can position you well for it."

"I think I understand."

"Consider for a moment your mother's bright blue teapot at home."

"Mom's teapot?"

"Yes. How is it used?"

"Well, she puts dried tea leaves in it, and pours hot water onto them, and makes tea to drink."

"That's right. Imagine the tea leaves as an opportunity. And think of the hot water as your energy, the effort that you pour into a situation of new opportunity."

"Ok."

In addition to the opportunity and the energy, you need something like a teapot—a structure or container, in order to make the tea successfully, and hold it, and pour it into cups, to share with others, as well as for your own enjoyment."

Walid smiled and said, "Yes, that's true."

"These seven conditions of success create a metaphorical teapot. And remember what else is needed. There has to be an opportunity. No tea leaves, no tea. And there must be energy poured in. The hot water of good effort is also necessary. But these seven conditions, or guides, provide a structure, something like a vessel of transformation, whereby and wherein a great result can be produced. The teapot itself can't guarantee great tea. But it facilitates the process and the achievement."

"That's a wild comparison."

Ali laughed. "Yes, perhaps it is. But it may help with your memory of what I'm saying, and your understanding."

"It makes me thirsty."

And at that, the old man laughed again.

The boy now sat up, smiling. He hesitated for a moment and grew serious once more, and then said, "I was thinking about what Masoon recently taught me with his principle of The Triple Double."

"Yes?"

"And he used the concept of a toolkit—a toolkit of ideas."

"He did."

"So. What's the relationship between that toolkit of ideas and the thoughts on success that you've given to me just now?"

Ali smiled and said, "This is a good question, my avid student. Do you remember every part of The Triple Double?"

"I do. Whenever I face the possibility of serious trouble, I have to engage in a triple double—three pairs of actions— Prepare and Perceive; Anticipate and Avoid; Concentrate, and Control."

"Excellent! You recall perfectly. The Triple Double is a protective tool. It's all about first avoiding whatever trouble in this world you can elude, and then dealing with any you must face. The seven conditions of success, by contrast, are tools for creating the future that you want and need, or simply attaining any desired goal at hand. These two different frameworks of ideas are obviously related and are mutually supporting. But they're also distinct. Pondering their relationship will give you a full command of what they offer. But it's something that will be good for you to do, yourself."

"I see, I think." Walid now smiled and said.

"Good. When you take time to explore ideas, you come to a new level of understanding and command over them."

Walid thought for a moment more, and then said, "Mom and dad have always taught me important things about life and the world. But I feel like this trip is really speeding up my education."

"The time is right, my friend."

"You've given me so much to think about since our visit to the first oasis."

"And you'll have much to do with all these insights, quite soon, as you put them to work. It's my wish that the thoughts and lessons I've been able to pass on to you will assist greatly in what's to come."

"I feel much more prepared already. I just hope that what I do will always reflect the best of what I know."

"That's a wise perspective, my boy, and a hope that's good for any of us to have. We need to remind ourselves. Wisdom is a matter of insights and actions, never just of words alone. Anyone can say the words. Only a truly wise person will do the deeds that the words suggest. In this world, a thinker must be a doer, and a doer must be a thinker, or things will never go as well as they could."

He paused for a moment and then said, "Now, perhaps a short nap wouldn't hurt. In fact, it can be beneficial in more than one way. Did you know that a bit of sleep after learning something new helps us to retain what we've heard?"

"I didn't know that," Walid said as he lay back but still leaned up on one elbow.

"Well, perhaps you'll best remember these seven secrets, as well as this new little piece of information about memory, if you now sleep on it all, however briefly. Then we'll continue our travel."

"I'd like that. And so I'll engage in three more conditions right now, conditions that sound to me a bit like your seven."

"What is it that you mean, my boy?" The old man smiled again, since at this point he knew to anticipate something clever from his nephew.

"I'll collapse, curl-up, and conk-out!" Walid suddenly fell back onto the blanket and closed his eyes for dramatic effect.

"Good! Me, too!" Ali laughed with the boy, and both grew quiet until the drowsiness of mid-day sleep overtook them. Important things were soon to come that would indeed require a command of all the wisdom available.

14

THE GIFT OF UNCERTAINTY

THE EVENING MEAL WAS LATE, DUE TO THE EXTENDED TRAVEL OF THE DAY.

And the time for eating was then all a bit rushed. After dinner, the men sat in small clusters around their temporary camp, conferring about the events of the past twenty-four hours, and planning things to come. Masoon and the doctor Hamid seemed to be leading different groups in discussion and preparation. Hakeem had also convened a small gathering.

Walid walked among the groups, staying quietly outside their circles, and listening for the snatches of conversation he could overhear. Phrases like 'without loss of life, if possible' and 'fast and silent' floated on the air. There was an atmosphere of intense concentration throughout the camp. Almost everyone was speaking at some point or other, and they all seemed to be in agreement as they divided up their respective responsibilities and laid out some new details of what should happen once they were in the city.

Lots of thoughts ran through Walid's head as he walked around. He still had a swirl of emotions about all the new revelations and what was now playing out so quickly, and some of his thoughts and feelings fought with others, as he tried to stay positive amid all the uncertainties that tugged at him. Concerns now began engaging him in ways that reflected the conversation he had earlier in the day with his uncle. He said to himself, "I need to set some goals. I need a clear conception of what I want—Ok. I want to get through this revolution safely and I want Uncle Ali to be king, like he's supposed to be. I want mom and dad to know what's going on, soon. I want the plan about Faisul to work. I want Bancom to get to our friends in time. And I want to be a good prince for the kingdom—whatever that means."

Just as he was going over these things in his mind, it suddenly occurred to Walid that he was perhaps not in fact setting any goals at all, but simply expressing to himself various important wishes and desires that he felt. And at that moment, he saw Ali arise from one of the circles not far away, bid the others a good night, and begin to make his way toward their tent.

Walid jogged over to catch up with him and called out, "Uncle, can I speak with you for a minute?"

"Certainly, my boy." The old man turned with a smile to face Walid and as he drew close, he reached out a hand to take hold of his shoulder. "What can I do for you this evening, Your Highness?"

"You don't have to call me that." Walid looked a bit embarrassed.

"No, but it may be good for you to grow accustomed to it." Ali kept his smile.

"I guess so. But I have a question."

"Yes. Good. I have several at any given time." The boy smiled at these words, and so did the rightful king who had just voiced them, and who then said, "Anything you need or want to know, just ask. Let's walk as we talk."

"Ok. Great. I'd like to learn something more about goals."

"What do you have in mind?"

"Well, I was just thinking about some of the things I want to see happen in the coming days, and I believed at first that I was setting some new goals, but then it seemed to me that maybe I was just expressing wishes to myself, and that's not likely the same thing."

"No, it's not. Could you give me an example?"

"Sure. I thought to myself that I want you to be king soon, and I want the plan about Faisul to work, and for Bancom to get to the city in time to set things in motion for us."

"I see. You have all good wishes in these words. I want those things to happen, too. And I often set myself personal goals based on such desires. But, for you, they can all seem to be things that are just too far outside your power to bring about, or even to act on at present."

Walid nodded. He said, "That was part of what bothered me."

Ali nodded and replied, "You should understand first that there's absolutely no problem about having wants and wishes concerning things that are far beyond your power—we all have legitimate desires about how things should go, in all sorts of ways, and that's a good thing. Our desires can often suggest real goals. But to set for yourself a genuine goal, you must envision something very clear and specific in the future, however remote or immediate, which you can begin to act on helping to bring about, and you have to commit yourself to it."

"Could you explain more to me about how that's done?"

"Easily. Consider our beloved Rumi. Your father once felt a growing sense of mission to help the sick and injured, and so set himself the goal of becoming a medical doctor. Then he asked what it would take to reach that goal. He talked to people, read a lot, and figured out some intermediate goals and then more immediate ones that would lead to his desired destination. Then, he set out to achieve those smaller aims, one after another and, as a result, he moved steadily in the direction of his ultimate intent. And so, he finally attained his big goal by achieving lots of smaller ones first."

"But Uncle, how can I set any such goals now, in the present situation, about these things that are suddenly happening? I'm still so young, and most of what's going on is far outside my power to affect."

"Well, ask yourself a question. What is within your power to affect? You can decide, for example, to act right now in a supporting role for the men. You can commit yourself to being alert to whatever is needed by those who are working around us, and then doing anything you can to help meet those needs."

"Ok. I see."

"For instance, I have some maps in our tent that Hakeem wants to consult later. You could take them to him when we finish speaking. One of your goals could be to provide quick and flawless assistance to me, to our other leaders, and to all our friends, whenever possible."

"I can do that."

"Good. In pursuing the goal of being a great assistant right now, a servant to others, you'll be learning more about the men and the mission we're on. All of that will be important to know in the near future, and may help you to set and attain other appropriate goals." He paused for a moment and then continued. "There's an old Chinese saying that's very wise: 'The loftiest towers start from the ground.' Do you understand?"

"I'm not sure. What does it mean?"

"Noble goals can be attained from humble beginnings. We start where we are, use what we have, and move forward from there."

Walid replied, "I like that thought. Can I then also set goals for things that are more in the future, like my father did?"

"Yes. You can indeed set goals for your future, and you should. If you want to be a good prince, and later a good king, you can find out what that requires, and busy yourself with supporting goals that lead in this direction. The title of prince will be yours, if things go as planned. It's rightfully yours already. But the real job it involves will be something you must grow into through your own goals and self-development —that is, if you choose to continue to accept this role and opportunity."

"I want to," Walid said. "I really do. It strikes me as right, like you've said a proper next adventure should. But I just don't know yet what all it involves."

"It's often like this in life. We find ourselves in a new position, or role, or status that's been given to us, for whatever reason. It's then up to us, often more than we realize, to decide what we'll make of it. And that can happen only through investigation and discovery and thoughtful self-examination, along with the right goal setting and personal initiative."

"But what if I set the wrong goals in pursuit of what I want, goals that aren't really right for me?"

"Then, in pursuing them, you'll likely come to realize that —you'll recognize the problem, and you will, in the process, have put yourself into a better position to see what other goals would instead be more appropriate. Life is an exploration full of experiments. It's a process of learning and adapting to what we learn."

They had now come to their tent. While Ali held open the flap for his nephew, the boy looked very serious and, as he ducked into their humble abode, he spoke up with a related concern.

"I have one big problem, and attached to it, a worry."

Ali followed and sat down with him. He asked, "What's that?"

Walid answered, "When I try to imagine the future, even next week, there's so much uncertainty about it all. And this really bothers me."

"Don't worry. Such is the world. And this is everyone's condition, whether they realize it or not. Each of us is a work of art in progress, and so is our journey together. Uncertainty is the canvas on which all our lives are painted. There are many intermediate points of certainty in life, and some large scale universals, but for the most part, we play out our destinies against a backdrop of many unknowns."

"To be honest, Uncle, I think that uncertainty and the unknown sometimes really scare me, deep down."

"You're like most other people in feeling initially uneasy or even fearful about the unknown. And there's nothing wrong with that. It's natural. But then, the crucial question is, what will you do with your fear? Will you allow it to stop you? Will you give it the power to make your life small? Or will you thank it for its cautions, acknowledge its causes, investigate its concerns, and then move forward with it as your sometimes-useful advisor, but not the ruler of your heart?"

"I've never thought about it like this."

"That's what courage is. A courageous man feels fear, but doesn't follow all the orders barked out by this one emotion. He listens, and even consults its concerns. But, most of all, in the end, he does what he thinks is right, despite any fear he may feel."

"So, brave people can feel scared?"

"Yes. But the more they act bravely, the weaker the fear becomes."

"That's a really helpful insight."

"Good. And now I have another thought for you, a big one."

"What is it?"

"Consider the possibility that uncertainty is a gift."

Walid actually laughed. "What do you mean, Uncle? That's a very surprising thing to say."

Now the old man had a special sparkle in his eye, and spoke with great conviction.

"It may be that uncertainty makes possible many of the best things in life. Think about it for a moment. There's a sense in which uncertainty and the unknown provide us with the possibility of possibility, and so with ample room to dream and do as we desire. Without the open future they give us, our souls couldn't truly grow. These conditions establish the arena within which we can be original and creative. They also allow us to develop the important quality of faith, as well as an inwardly formed personal confidence, not in the easy way that simple certainty would give, but in a way that makes these characteristics genuine personal accomplishments."

Walid spoke up and said, "I've never thought about uncertainty like that."

"Most people don't. But now consider something else, my friend: Perhaps we're in this world to throw our own special lights into the darkness and illumine a path for ourselves as well as others. Without that darkness, we'd have no real work to do. Uncertainty allows for heroic effort, productive action, and distinctively human achievement. This condition that we tend to dislike and regret and even fear may be the thing that allows us to do and become all that we most admire."

"Wow. These are completely new perspectives for me."

"I'm glad I can provide new things for you to think about tonight, and as you ponder potential goals for the future. Don't allow any worries about uncertainty, and all that's unknown in life, to hold you back. We all face the same fog-shrouded field of action. Think of the unknown and the uncertain as making possible the most exciting challenges and opportunities that you need in order to develop and grow and become the best you can be. The secret is to embrace the always open future as your creative playground, your own experimental laboratory, and as the place in which you can do your most fulfilling personal work. In an open field, we can choose many paths."

"But why does almost everyone seem to seek certainty all the time, if uncertainty is so important?"

"The answer to your question is simple. And it's sad. Most people don't know what they truly need, because they don't know who they really are. If they could even glimpse their own potential greatness, and understand how far they are from where they can go, and what they can become, they'd view the uncertainties and open possibilities of life very differently, and perhaps as I suggest."

"I see." Walid sat for a moment and then said, "So, it's all right for me to set goals for myself, despite the many uncertainties to come?"

Ali laughed and replied, "It's important for you to set goals precisely because of the many uncertainties to come!"

"That's wild. I was looking at it all backwards!" The boy shook his head and thought for a few more seconds. Then, he said, "I always love talking with you about things like this, Uncle. You give me new ways of looking at life. And you often show me that I've been thinking about something in the opposite way from what's best."

Ali laughed again. He said, "That's how it goes for all of us. We tend to get things wrong before we get them right. But then we most often remember better what we've learned when we do see the truth."

The old man patted the boy gently on his arm, as they now sat on their blankets. "Life is full of surprises. That's a part of what makes it so rich and interesting and good."

Walid smiled. "I'll think more about what you've told me. But right now, I need to get those maps to Hakeem so that he'll be able to guide us better into the uncertain unknown that awaits us."

"Are you certain, my boy?"

Walid laughed in surprise at his uncle's question, and they both enjoyed the little joke, as they often did in their times together. A lot that was going on, and that was yet to come, was uncertain. But Walid had a thought, right then, a sudden anticipation or inkling, that many great things may lie ahead. He had no idea of the unexpected dangers he would soon face, and the astonishing people he would meet. He could not have guessed at even a small fraction of what was to come, and very quickly—not even in his wildest imagination.

Much was yet to be revealed.

APPENDIX

The Diary of Walid Shabeezar
In the Desert

Uncle Ali has been teaching me some important things about life. I decided to write a few notes about them here to help me understand and not forget. I should have been keeping a diary for the whole journey. I could have written about what I learned from the desert itself even before these lessons began. The world is one big classroom. It's good to take notes. Writing helps me think. When I see mom and dad next, I'll share these notes with them.

△ △ △

An oasis is fun, safe, and relaxing. We can carry an oasis within us wherever we go, an inner place of calm and refreshment, by using our thoughts well.

We all have in our minds something like an emotional telescope. If we look through the end everyone uses, things will seem bigger than they really are. But we can flip it around and look through the other end. That will make things appear smaller and less threatening. So whenever anything looks big and overwhelming, say to yourself, "Flip the telescope!"

Almost anything needs interpretation. That's where freedom begins.

Whether something is a big deal or not often turns on how we see it. If you think it's a big deal, it is. But you can change your mind on many things and shrink them down to size.

Wisdom for life is about seeing things properly. It's about perspective. This gives us power, because it brings peace to our hearts, and then we can think clearly, even in difficult times.

If I live most fully with my heart and mind in the reality of the present moment, I will feel better and be more effective.

△ △ △

We all need a healthy, dynamic balance in our lives. Too much of anything gets us out of balance. And that requires change.

There's no such thing as perfect balance. In this world, balance is just an ongoing dance of correction and adjustment.

Whatever I do, I should do with all my heart, putting aside distraction and second-guessing.

It's vital to listen to our deepest feelings about what's appropriate, and when a change is needed.

We should never let temporary feelings lead to big or permanent changes.

In very important matters, only our deepest feelings, together with our strongest values, can guide us properly.

Commitments and promises allow us to live well and work helpfully with others.

Δ Δ Δ

Things are not always what they seem. In fact, they often aren't.

Whenever life brings us a storm, we should use what we have, stay calm, and move quickly to respond well.

An oasis within us is a place of peace and power in our hearts.

We can learn the most from the most difficult things.

We can't control the day, but only what we make of the day.

We should always try to make the best of whatever comes our way.

Δ Δ Δ

Many things have two powers—they can be helpful or harmful. It's often up to us which role they play.

Most situations also have a double potential, for good or ill. We would be wise to keep that in mind.

It's important in life to pay attention all the time—to look, listen, and learn.

We should discipline our thoughts and feelings, then listen when they suggest that something's not right.

Most dangers in the world will provide us with some kind of warning, if we're alert and aware.

Emotions, like most other things, can help us or harm us. We need to learn when to act on them, and when to resist them for a greater good.

△ △ △

We're all born into a royalty of the mind. We're meant to rule well over our thoughts and feelings. We can reject this, or embrace it.

Anyone who acts with nobility and humility can expand his kingdom from the mind outward into the world.

Nobility is a sense of our own greatness, and the greatness of our mission in life.

Humility is a recognition that there's greatness in others, and is an open-ness to learn from them.

Nobility comes from within us. We decide whether to bring it to whatever we do and experience.

Humility is also a choice. It's a decision to view ourselves properly, and to grow in all good ways.

More is possible for our lives and for what we can accomplish than we ever might imagine.

△ △ △

Unless you're very strong, or have many strong friends with you, you should be cautious about isolated places, where thieves prefer to strike. Alone, we're vulnerable. Together, we're strong.

Most battles are won or lost in the mind before any manifestation in the world.

Great things are accomplished by great thoughts. Our thoughts can be very powerful.

A good attitude about difficulties, combined with a wise perspective, can help us overcome any trouble.

We should be more surprised when things don't change than when they do. If we expect change, we can deal with it better.

We shouldn't worry about what we can't control. We should focus on what we can control and make the best of it.

Most people are afraid to enlarge their thoughts and make room for the miracles that could happen to them. They prefer the small circle of what they already know, and they endure shrunken lives as a result.

Many fear their own inner power, and so never draw on it well. What's really to be feared is missing out on the best life has to offer. And our deepest inner resources provide for that.

It's important to live fully each day.

△ △ △

Much wisdom comes from paying attention to what we see and hear in the world, reading good books, talking with wise people, and thinking about it all.

Thinking is hard work that, when done well, pays off.

Thinking insightfully is a skill that can only be learned by trying.

Some wisdom is mysterious and seems to fall like rain from heaven. It can happen any time and at any place. When this rain comes, it's crucial to have a good, strong wisdom bucket in your heart to catch the insights and retain them well.

Whenever we feel wisdom come to us, we should open ourselves to the new thoughts it may bring.

If I keep my wisdom bucket filled, others will come to me for a drink. I should also seek out those who themselves have full buckets. From such people, I can learn great things.

Wisdom is for everyone. True wisdom is to be lived and shared.

Wisdom isn't about what you say; it's mostly about how you live.

Wisdom is a way of life. It's a matter of how you think, act, and feel.

Our deepest desires come to us as signs of who we are and what we can do. If we want something with all our heart, from the innermost places inside us, we can be sure this desire is leading us to where we need to go, and to what we need to learn.

A book that's not worth reading twice wasn't worth reading once.

Those who seek wisdom will find it. But living too busy and hectic a life can keep you from discovering it.

△ △ △

The ancients believed that there are four elements from which everything comes: earth, air, water, and fire.

The earth gives us our bodies, and our materials for life, shelter, and creativity. It can allow us to move forward, or present a difficult path.

The air gives us breath and information, help, refreshment, and sometimes, resistance and storms.

Water is the elixir of life. It supports living things and growth, but can also bring damage and death.

Fire is the basic energy of creation, transformation, and destruction. Both physical fire and spiritual fire are behind creative generation, movement, and the warmth that refreshes and inspires.

The flame of high purpose, the fire of the spirit within us, can burn through any obstacle, if we let it grow.

When I encounter difficulties and problems, I should think to myself, "More fuel for the fire."

As we cultivate the fire within us, we can provide needed heat, light, and energy to those around us who need it. Others will be attracted to our flame, and can be sparked into action with us.

△ △ △

All four elements—earth, air, water, and fire—dwell in each of us physically. They're also in our hearts. But there's usually one that dominates in a person.

A fire person is full of passion. Many creators and warriors are fire people.

An earth person is solid and dependable, a hard worker who can be trusted. Earth people care about details and cultivate their skills.

A water person flows out to those who are in need and nourishes them, replenishing them, and helping them sail on to success.

An air person communicates information well and moves to connect people and bring things into our lives that are needed and useful.

Sometimes, two of the four elements can equally, or almost equally, lead in a person. In rare cases, three may govern together.

If we know the main element or group of elements that predominates in a person, or the one that may be most lacking, we can relate to him better and have more reasonable expectations of him, or her.

Each of the four elements can bring great good or great harm. It's our job to live with them well and make our own choices as to how they should appear in and through us.

△ △ △

Exercise is the main cause of personal growth—for mind and body. I need to engage in a daily exercise of both.

To deal with trouble, use The Triple Double: Prepare, Perceive; Anticipate, Avoid; Concentrate, and Control.

We should prepare our bodies and minds for any extreme and challenging circumstances we might face. Preparation helps us navigate our world.

A completely aware and perceptive person is seldom completely surprised.

Those who anticipate difficulty can best respond to it.

The easiest way of dealing with most potential troubles is to avoid them.

A disciplined concentration of our minds will set us apart from most people who might threaten to harm us.

The ability to exercise some control over your self and your situation is crucial for overcoming trouble.

The worst times in our lives can make possible the best times.

△ △ △

I'm a prince—a real prince. I'll one day be a king.

I had to write that down to remind myself it's true. It's still hard to believe. But I'm willing to do my job, whatever it might require.

My dream is now a destiny. Being a prince or a king is not about rights. It's about responsibilities. I'll be available and responsible and brave. I'll be noble and humble. And I'll follow the lead of Uncle Ali. I admire him and trust him completely. We can do great things together. And we'll help others to do great things. I can't wait to talk to my parents about all of this!

We should think about how to react if challenging things happen. By creative anticipation and reasonable planning, we can often turn what's unfortunate into something fortunate.

There's a war in the world between goodness and corruption, between true love and uncontrolled lust. Goodness and love will prevail in the end. That's the best hope and philosophy we have.

We'll each have many adventures, both good and challenging, and they'll all help us move into the future.

△ △ △

When we face difficult things, it's better to plan than worry.

Anxiety is corrosive. It erodes the soul. It adds nothing positive.

Our destiny is the combined fruit of what happens to us and what happens because of us.

There are seven universal conditions for success in anything we do. We need to start with a clear Conception of what we want, launch out with a strong Confidence, maintain a focused Concentration, work with a stubborn Consistency, keep an emotional Commitment to what we're doing, guide our actions with good Character, and cultivate a Capacity to Enjoy the process along the way.

These secrets can't promise us success, but they can position us for it.

The seven conditions are at first a test for setting proper goals, and then a tool for attaining them. They can also be a diagnostic device for locating the source of a problem, when things aren't quite right.

A goal is a decision, a commitment of the will. Anything less is just a fantasy, or a mere wish.

I hope that what I do will always honor what I know and value.

The purpose of wisdom is to be lived in the world.

△ △ △

I should never worry about what I can't do, but focus on what I can do, and set personal goals that start there.

Lofty towers rise from the ground. Great things can come from humble starting points.

Uncertainty often bothers me and brings a tinge of fear, but Uncle Ali had good advice about this.

Fear can make a life small. I should never allow that to happen.

Fear is natural. But courage feels it and then does what's right.

Uncertainty is the canvas on which all our lives are painted.

Consider the possibility that uncertainty is a gift.

Darkness in life allows us to bring light and make a difference.

Faith and confidence can be personal accomplishments when we face the unknown.

The open future offers me a field for creativity, a place of experiment, and meaningful work to do.

Most people don't know what they truly need because they don't know who they really are.

The uncertainties of life don't just make goal-setting possible, they make it necessary.

Life is full of surprises.

△ △ △

A heart full of faith is the most important thing in life.

Whatever happens next, I'm ready to do my part. Whatever life brings, I'll have my oasis within.

The oasis within is a place of strength and positive possibility.

I'll remember these images and their lessons:

The telescope and emotion
The tightrope and balance
The tempest and learning
The treasure and power
The tube of changing patterns
The tiger and greatness
The toolkit and trouble
The teapot and success

May the future bring us great things and ample opportunities to do good for others!

ACKNOWLEDGMENTS

MANY PEOPLE HAVE ENCOURAGED ME IN THE WRITING OF THIS BOOK. My wise and loving wife, Mary Morris, has cheered on the process and asked interesting questions at every stage along the way. Going far beyond the normal spousal involvement, she let me read the first draft of the book to her out loud, once chapters were done, and while it was still being written. Her comments were always helpful and meant a lot.

My daughter, the multi-talented Sara Morris, worked wonders with our cover art. Her eye for design is great. And we all deeply appreciate the design expertise and faithful efforts of Abigail Chiaramonte, who brought all the elements together, inside and out. Many thanks to them both.

My friends and fellow philosophers Dave Baggett and Jerry Walls read early drafts, as did Rich Boyd, Steve Leveen, David McWilliams, Don Sharp, Tom Ryder, and Ed Hearn, along with a few other friends. I thank them all for their tremendous encouragement. Ed truly championed the process at every stage, encouraged me with enthusiasm all along the way, and saved me from numerous typos and convoluted sentences, except, of course, for this one. When Steve, who is the highly astute co-founder and chairman of Levenger, read the first draft, it was only six chapters long. I had thought that was the whole thing, and it was an extremely short story. He asked me, "Is this the whole book?" I said, "Yes." He then said "No. I don't think so. There are things yet to happen." And so I waited. More chapters came. And now, nearly a million words and seven more much longer books later, all unexpected sequels to the small tale here, I realize how importantly right he was. And it was because of an email Tom Ryder wrote me that I decided to include at the end of this book, and all the others, passages from Walid's Diary, apparently found years after the events recorded here.

The incidents in this book and their lessons have been of immense help to me in focusing my own thoughts for the challenges and opportunities that life brings every day. I hope they'll be helpful in similar ways for you.

This book is dedicated to all my fellow travelers in search of more wisdom, and especially to the friends named above, who have helped inspire me to think big, listen well, and tell some of the story in my heart. Most of all, I dedicate it to my granddaughter, Grayson.

I also want to thank all the friends who have already asked me what will come next for Walid, Ali, and their companions. You'll soon find out. There are amazing adventures ahead for us.

The events and conversations recorded here came to me on their own terms, suddenly and unexpectedly, like a very vivid movie in my head. After the first chapter came to me unbidden on the very first day of this adventure, I took up a daily practice. I made myself quiet and sat calmly, and then on most days the story would start up and take many surprising turns that I never saw coming. But you'll see.

This book is the prologue to the most amazing developments yet to come. I had no idea what would happen next. And I found myself astonished, time after time, as the movie I needed to watch played on.

Last, but not least, I thank you, the reader, for your time and care. I hope you've enjoyed what's here, and I also hope that you'll experience a measure of my own joy in what's going to happen next, and next, and then after that.

Wilmington, NC

First draft, Winter, 2011
Final draft, Spring 2015

"Oh, you have traveled far."
"Yes, I have gained my experience."
\- As You Like It

AFTERWORD
Beyond the Oasis

This book is a prologue and companion volume to an exciting new series of novels entitled:

WALID AND THE MYSTERIES OF PHI

If you've enjoyed this book, you'll likely love the series, which presents a sprawling epic story of action and adventure, set in and around Egypt in 1934 and 1935, with a few sojourns farther abroad. Its seven books contain captivating tales about life, death, meaning, love, friendship, the deepest secrets behind everyday events, and the extraordinary power of a well-focused mind. With unexpected humor and continual intrigue, you'll gradually discover in these books the outlines of a powerful worldview and a profound philosophy of life.

To find out more, visit **www.TomVMorris.com/novels** or go to **www.TheOasisWithin.com**.

This companion book, *The Oasis Within*, is available for large group purchases at special discounts. To find out more, contact the author, Tom Morris, through his email address, **TomVMorris@aol.com**.

CPSIA information can be obtained at www.ICGtesting.com
Printed in the USA
BVOW05*1746300516

449848BV00001B/2/P